# Escape from Hell

### By

I0637772

### G.S. Willmott

# Contents

# INTRODUCTION

Wars are usually fought over territory, natural resources or religious differences whatever the reason they have created, changed or destroyed entire nations. The oldest profession in the world is the military the second oldest profession followed the armies on their conquests. War reaches back to the beginning of mankind although the first recorded war occurred in 2700 B.C. The belligerents were Sumer (in modern Iraq) and Elam (a region that is now part of Iran) This conflict was fought in the area around Basra in Iraq. Of course, tribes, cities, etc., had been fighting each other for thousands of years before that, but there are no written records of these earlier conflicts.

Prisoners of War (POW) helped establish and build nations such as Egypt, Rome, Athens and the Persian Empire. All these nations and cities rose or fell on the strength of their armies.

The dictionary definition of Prisoner of War is:

"A prisoner of war (POW) enemy prisoner of war (EPW) or Missing-Captured is a person, whether combatant or non-combatant, who is held in custody by an enemy power during or immediately after an armed conflict."

The earliest recorded usage of the phrase is dated 1660.


For most of human history depending on the culture of the victors, combatants on the losing side in a battle could expect to be either slaughtered or enslaved.

The first Roman gladiators were prisoners of war and were named according to their ethnic roots such as Samnite, Thracian and the Gaul. Homer's Iliad describes Greek and Trojan soldiers offering rewards of wealth to enemies who have defeated them on the battlefield in exchange for mercy, their offers were not always accepted.

In the later Middle Ages, a number of religious wars aimed to not only defeat but also eliminate their enemies. In Christian Europe, the extermination of the heretics or "non-believers" was considered their main objective. Examples include the 13th century Albigensian Crusade and the Northern Crusades. When asked by a Crusader how to distinguish between the Catholics and Cathars once they'd taken the city of Béziers, the Papal Legate Arnaud Amalric famously replied, "Kill them all, God will know His own".

Likewise the inhabitants of conquered cities were frequently massacred during the Crusades against the Muslims in the 11th and 12th centuries. Noblemen could hope to be ransomed; their families would have to send to their captors large sums of money depending on their social status.

Many French prisoners of war were killed during the Battle of Agincourt in 1415

In feudal Japan there was no custom for ransoming prisoners of war, who were for the most part summarily executed

Every city or town that refused surrender and resisted the Mongols was subject to destruction

The Aztecs were constantly at war with neighbouring tribes and groups. The goal of this constant warfare was to collect live prisoners for sacrifice.

In pre-Islamic Arabia, upon capture, those captives not executed were made to beg for their subsistence. During the early reforms under Islam, Muhammad changed this custom and made it the responsibility of the Islamic government to provide food and clothing on a reasonable basis to captives, regardless of their religion.

The freeing of prisoners in particular was highly recommended as a charitable act. Christians, who were captured during the Crusades, were usually either killed or sold into slavery if they could not pay a ransom.

After the Napoleonic wars between 1796 and 1797 a camp was built at Norman Cross near Peterborough in England to accommodate seven thousand French prisoners of war. This was the first purpose built POW camp; it was situated on a forty-acre tract of land. London was only 78 miles to the south by the Great North Road.

This book covers POWs who escaped as well as the prisoners who escaped from the cruel and sadistic German death camps. Now it's the Russians turn.

So began the era of escape.

# CIVIL UNREST

## CHAPTER 1

At the outbreak of the Civil War in 1861, Luther Libby was running a ship supply store from the corner of a large warehouse in Richmond, Virginia. The building had been used as a tobacco factory prior to Libby taking possession. In need of a new prison for captured Union officers, the Confederate Government gave Libby 48 hours to evacuate his property. The sign over the northwest corner reading "L. Libby & Son, Ship Chandlers" was never removed, and consequently the building and prison bore his name. Since the Confederates believed the building was escape proof, the prison guards considered their job relatively straightforward.

Most people around the globe have assumed the Civil War occurred because the North was no longer willing to tolerate slavery as being part of the structure of U.S. society and that the political power brokers in Washington were planning to abolish slavery throughout the Union. Therefore, for most people, slavery was the fundamental issue in explaining the causes of the American Civil War.

It's not quite that simple; slavery was a major issue but not the only factor in pushing America into a horrendous bloody conflict.

By April 1861 the slavery issue had been entwined with other major issues such as state rights. The southern states objected to the fact that the Federal Government was dictating what was wrong and what was right. These southerners felt their whole way of life was changing for the worse and they didn't like it.

All these issues contributed to the American Civil War.

By 1860 America could not be seen as one society. The North and the South were like two separate counties, each with their own value systems and interpretation of the rule of law.

It became North versus South, The Union versus The Confederates: WAR.

The South was agrarian; cotton and tobacco were the main backbone to the region's economic strength. The southern states relied on exports to markets in Western Europe. The class structure in Britain was mimicked in the south. The local plantation owner was a 'Baron' within his own domain; the local population would be deferential towards such men. The South constituted a strictly Christian society that had a hierarchy of men at the top while those underneath were expected and required to accept their social status. Social advancement for the less privileged was possible but unusual; invariably one advanced within the senior families who were the economic, political and legal brokers of their state.

Certainly the wealth created by the plantation owners relied heavily on slave labour and was accepted in the south as the natural way of doing things.

If slave labour were no longer available to them their wealth would have been seriously affected. It was not only the barons who would suffer but also the local communities that relied on their support would have suffered.

When the dogs of war began to howl in 1860-61, many in the South saw their very way of life being threatened. Part of that included slavery, but it was not the only part.

The North's way of life was diametrically opposed to the South; it had become an industrial powerhouse and was growing at an incredible pace.

In the North you did not need to be born into a wealthy family. Many poor boys became entrepreneurs, such as Samuel Colt who died a multi-millionaire.

Cornelius Vanderbilt was another example. Whether an immigrant from the Netherlands could have made his way into the social hierarchy of the South is open to debate. The North was also a cosmopolitan mixture of nationalities and religions – far more so than the South. There can be little doubt that there were important groups in the North that were anti-slavery and wanted its abolition throughout the Union. However, there were also groups that were ambivalent and those who knew that the North's economic development was based not only on entrepreneurial skills but also on the input of poorly paid workers who were not slaves but lived lives not totally removed from those in the South. While they had their freedom and were paid, their lifestyle was at best very harsh.

While the belligerents of the American Civil War were opposed in many areas, it became worse with the perception in the South that the North would try to impose its own values on their beloved land.

In 1832, South Carolina passed an act declaring Federal tariff legislation could not be enforced onto states. This meant after February 1st 1833 the tariffs would not be recognised in South Carolina. This brought the rogue State into direct conflict with the Federal government in Washington DC.

Congress passed the "Force Bill" enabling the President to use military force to bring any state into line with regards to implementing Federal law. On this occasion the threat of military force worked, South Carolina capitulated.

It was at this time slavery became entwined with state rights. The question was: how much power had a state compared to Federal authority? The key issue was whether slavery would be allowed to continue in the newly created States that were joining the Union?

This dispute escalated when the federal government purchased Kansas. The new state was officially opened for settlement in 1854, when both pro-slavery and anti-slavery settlers poured in, setting up a scenario of violence and acrimony.

On January 29th 1861, Kansas was admitted to the Union as a slave-free state. Many in the traditional slave states of the South saw this as the first step towards abolishing slavery throughout the Union and thus the destruction of their southern way of life.

South Carolina seceded from the Union on December 20th 1860, the first state to do so; it felt it was being dominated by a Federal Government, which was controlled by the North. Whether this was true or not, is not relevant as it was felt to be true by many South Carolinians. The secession of South Carolina pushed other southern states into doing the same. With such a background of distrust between most southern states and the Government in Washington, it only needed one incident to set off a civil war and that occurred at Fort Sumter in April 1861.

**Fort Sumter**

The attack on Fort Sumter began on Friday, April 12 1861 It is seen as the start of the American Civil War.

In 1860, a Federal grant of $80,000 was given to complete the construction of Fort Sumter, as it had lain unfinished for a number of years.

The fort was constructed to hold a garrison of 650 men.

On 12 April 1861, General P.G.T. Beauregard of the Confederate forces attacked Fort Sumter. The fort housed three 10-inch guns placed to cover all the important angles. The fort also housed 8-inch columbiads, 42lbs, 32lbs and 24lbs guns and some 8-inch sea howitzers. Fort Sumter had its own fresh water supply and a hospital.

All hell was about to break loose: 625,000 people would lose their lives, many of them children.

Union Columbiad

It was not fully manned when it was attacked but still held out until April 22$^{nd}$ after more than 40,000 shells had been fired at her.

By the end of the war in <u>1865</u>, Fort Sumter was little more than a pile of rubble after constant shelling by Union forces.

## The Great Union Escape

Libby Prison

The Libby Prison Escape at Richmond, Virginia in February 1864 saw over one hundred Union prisoners-of-war escape from captivity. It was one of the most successful prison breaks of the American Civil War.

Led by Colonel Thomas E. Rose of the 77th Pennsylvania Infantry, the prisoners started tunnelling in a rat-infested area, which the Confederate guards were reluctant to enter. The tunnel emerged in a vacant lot beside a warehouse, from where the escapees could walk out through the gate without arousing suspicion. Since the prison was believed to be escape-proof, there was less vigilance by the authorities than in other camps, and the alarm was not raised for nearly twelve hours. Over half the prisoners were able to reach Union lines.

The complex was converted to a prison in March 1862 in response to problems at a prisoner depot in central Richmond. Located at Main and 25th streets, this facility had been established in 1861 after the first Union prisoners began pouring into Richmond following the Battle of Manassas on July 21. Its location made it difficult to secure, Confederate officials decided to occupy the Libby buildings because they were more secure. As the number of Union prisoners increased after the Seven Day Battles in June 1862, Libby Prison could not cope with the numbers and was therefore designated an officers-only facility.

Connected by thick inner doors, the three Libby buildings came to be known as East, Middle, and West. The Union POWs were confined to the upper two floors, which contained six sparsely furnished rooms; there were no bunks and few benches and each measured 105 by 45 feet. Wooden bars covered small windows, which offered no protection from the steaming heat in summer or bitter cold in winter. Little light permeated through these windows, making the cells a very dark inhospitable environment to live in. The kitchen was located on the first floor, Middle, and was the only room to which inmates had free access. The hospital was on the first floor, East, with offices and guardrooms on the first floor, West. The cellar was reserved for a carpenter shop and slave accommodation. The centre cellar had four solitary confinement cells reserved for troublemakers.

## Escape from Libby Prison

In late 1863, a group of Union officers began making plans to escape from the Confederate prison. They removed a stove located on the first floor and began digging their way into the adjoining building's chimney. The intending escapees constructed a tight but usable passage for access to the eastern basement. Having gained access to the basement, it was determined that a tunnel could be dug to Kerr's Warehouse to the east. From there they could escape into the street.

The escapees divided themselves into three digging squads comprising five men each. Using a broken shovel and two knives stolen from the kitchen for tools they began their endeavour. Most of their digging took place at night, as the Confederate guards were more likely to notice prisoners missing during daylight hours.

Digging the tunnel was not an easy task. Not only were they in complete darkness but the air was foul which made breathing difficult and, to top things off, the ubiquitous rats were constantly biting them as they worked.

When they had completed their tunnelling for the night they would cover over the entrance to the tunnel with a two-foot layer of straw. The guards never suspected a tunnel being dug right under their noses.

The officers' initial attempt came to an abrupt halt as they came across the foundations of the building. With the tools available to them, there was no way they could continue. They had to dig another tunnel, taking a different route and direction.

After tunnelling for a further twenty days they believed they had reached the desired exit point. They were wrong: the exit was directly next to a sentry box. They quickly covered it over and luckily were not detected.

The third and final attempt was successful. After thirty-eight days of digging, the men broke through to the surface, coming out in a storage shed of Kerr's Warehouse.

Colonel Thomas E. Rose, the escape leader, surveyed the location of the tunnel exit, and proclaimed to his diggers: 'The Underground Railroad to God's country is open!' Sometime after sundown on the night of February 9, 1864, Union officers began emerging from the tunnel in groups of two or three. They then began casually strolling through the front gate of the warehouse and headed north.

In all, one hundred and nine Federal officers emerged from the tunnel. It was not until late in the day of February 10 that repeated roll calls failed to account for the missing men. Frantic messages went out to local Confederate forces to apprehend the escapees. Nonetheless, over twelve hours passed before any Rebel response occurred.

# Aftermath

# THE SHOEMAKER

## CHAPTER 2

Tadeusz was a quiet lad who lived in the beautiful village of Kolaczyce in Poland. His father was a shoemaker as was his grandfather and great-grandfather before him.

It was expected that Tadeusz would follow the family tradition and in fact, he did. He was regarded as a very talented cordwainer and in much demand from the villagers. The town was quite small with a population of 1300 inhabitants. The town boasted a very significant Jewish population.

The village of Kolaczyce was founded in the late 13th century, as a benedictine abbey. In 1339, it received a town charter from King Kazimierz Wielki. At that time, it was declared part of Poland. In 1474, Kolaczyce was burned to the ground by a Hungarian raid commanded by Thomas Tarczay a general under King Matthias Corvinus. In 1546, the town burned in a great fire, while in 1657, it was completely destroyed by Transilvanian forces. It still remains part of Poland.

# 1940

The Germans and the Russians both invaded Poland in September 1939. Life for the Poles would never be the same. Tadeusz knew he and his family were at risk considering their Jewish faith.

Word had gotten out that the Germans had gathered 260 Jews from the nearby towns and marched them a few miles south along a forest road gathering them into groups of ten and escorting them into a clearing in the Podzamcze forest. Men women and children including babies were murdered and buried in a mass graves.

**Mass Murder by the Germans**

Tadeusz made the decision to leave his home and his village and join the underground to fight the Germans. His unit did cause some havoc but unfortunately, he was caught and arrested. He and 728 other prisoners were sent to the half-built Auschwitz.

# June 1940

Tadeusz was transported to Auschwitz concentration camp a place not yet known for its gas chambers, medical experiments and constant beatings but never the less, not a place you would want to be billeted.

He and the other 728 prisoners were tattooed with identification numbers. Tadeusz's number was 220; the last number tattooed on a prisoner was in May 1944, 450,000. The 12,000 Russian POWs were given different numbers.

Tadeusz was then escorted to his barracks hardly regarded as suitable accommodation.

Each day was a struggle for the Polish shoemaker barely surviving under unbearable conditions. He and the other prisoners were housed in primitive barracks that had no windows and were not insulated from the heat or cold. There was no bathroom, only a bucket. Each barrack held about 36 wooden bunk beds, and inmates were squeezed in five or six across on a wooden plank.

Although designed to hold 250 prisoners over 500 were crammed into these primitive buildings.

It didn't take long for Tadeusz to realise this place would be where he would take his last breath. He had seen fellow prisoners being beaten to death and others being shot for the most minor transgression. Several of the prisoners came from his village including his closest friend Jakob.

'Jakob we will both be dead before winter you know that don't you?'

'Yes my friend I'm aware of that but what can we do?'

'We can escape.'

'Are you mad Tadeusz there's electric fences around the entire perimeter and the place is crawling with sadistic SS guards. How do you propose to escape?'

'I don't know yet but I am determined to find a way Jakob.'

'Good luck with that my friend.'

'Does that mean you won't join me?'

'I'm hoping the war will end before winter and we can all walk out the front gate.'

'Good luck with that my friend.'

**Tadeusz and Jakob's barracks**

**Tadeusz Wiejowski**

Tadeusz along with many other prisoners was assigned to building brick two-story barracks to accommodate the prisoners arriving by train every day.

**Completed barracks**

Prisoners were employed as labourers to do the heavy work while outside tradesmen were used for the skilled work. These tradesmen would arrive in the morning and depart in the late afternoon.

Tadeusz worked closely with a team of electricians one of them came from Kolaczyce, Tadeusz's village they went to school together.

It was possible to have a conversation with the electricians without bringing on the wrath of the guards.

The shoemaker was able to discover that four of the tradesmen were members of the Polish underground including his friend Daniel.

'Daniel I want to escape from this hell hole would it be possible if you and the others help me?'

'I certainly would but I would have to ask my fellow workers. I'll let you know tomorrow.'

Daniel gave Tadeusz the good news the electricians would assist him to escape.


# July 6 1940

Daniel arrived at the barracks where the electricians were working. The SS guard escorting the prisoners sat down outside the building.

'Tadeusz at 3 pm come to me and I will give you a work suit, you will leave with us at 4 pm straight out the front gate.'

At 3pm Tadeusz approached the foreman Gideon who handed the young escapee his work suit. At 4pm the group of Polish electricians with toolboxes in hand walked casually out the gates from hell.

Once they were back in their village of Oswiecim Gideon took Tadeusz to his house where he was treated to a wonderful lamb stew with crusty bread.

The next morning he was given some money and was taken to the train station.

'Ok Tadeusz get into the freight carriage and stay hidden. You have a one-way ticket to Warsaw.'

'Ticket to Warsaw?'

'I'm joking no ticket just a freight cart.'

The first escapee from Auschwitz rode the freight train to what he hoped would be his freedom.

Tadeusz made a nest for himself from wool bales he hoped the German soldiers would just look into the carriage and see it was stacked with wool bales and move on. That was the plan.

The train would take five hours to get to Warsaw, Tadeusz fell asleep he woke as the train pulled into Warsaw train station.

German soldiers began searching all the freight carriages for stowaways.

Tadeusz lay still hardly breathing as two SS entered his carriage. They began to bayonet the bales a blade passed just in front of his nose. Satisfied the two Germans moved onto the next carriage.

The young escapee sighed a breath of relief. He had made it to Warsaw now all he had to do was get to Kolaczyce and his friends who he hoped would offer him refuge.


## The Price Paid

Each morning the prisoners were required to assemble in the front of their barracks for roll call.

It was soon established that one of the prisoners was missing, Tadeusz Wiejowski.

The prisoners were made to stand in assembly for many hours while SS guards beat and humiliated them to discover how the prisoner escaped. The Germans finally established who helped the Polish shoemaker escape.

The five Polish electricians were sentenced to death however, this was changed to imprisonment in Auschwitz the prison they helped to build. Four of the five died in the camp the one survivor died shortly after the war ended from injuries sustained in the camp.

Tadeusz returned to his village he decided to hide from the Germans in and around the area.

In the dead of night, he knocked on the door of his good friend's house.

The father of Antoni answered the door.

'What are you doing here Tadeusz I thought you had been captured by the Nazis and imprisoned.'

' Yes Mr Baranoski I was imprisoned in a concentration camp called Auschwitz It was a terrible place I knew if I didn't escape I would die.'

Antoni heard the voices and came out of his room to investigate.

'Tadeusz, I don't believe it how did you escape?'

' Hello Antoni It's a long story I'm very tired would you mind if I stayed here a while? I'll tell you all about it in the morning.'

'You can stay for a short while said Mr Baranoski but you will have to bunk up in the cellar the Germans patrol the village constantly and search houses randomly.'

Antoni took Tadeusz down to the cellar; it was cold and damp but never the less safe.

'I will bring you down some blankets and a pillow Tad'

In the meantime Antoni's mother had come down to see what was going on. Her husband Ludwik explained the situation. They both retired to their bedroom.

'You know that we will be imprisoned or even shot if the Germans discover we are harbouring an escapee?'

'Don't worry my love he will stay in the cellar no one will know he is here.'

'Well he can't stay here for ever a few weeks at the most.'

'Yes I agree Natalia, just a few weeks.'

In the first week Tad was fed in the basement it was a lonely existence even though Antoni was a regular visitor.

As time passed the family became more confident and Tadeusz was invited to eat his evening meal with the family.

The months went by and Tadeusz was still living in the cellar during November the family agreed that their houseguest could take a walk outside in the town square disguised as a woman.

Unfortunately, a Nazi collaborator recognised him from school and reported the cross-dresser to the Germans.

That night while sitting around the kitchen table six soldiers, all SS banged on the front door demanding entry. There was no time to retreat to the cellar even if there had been time they would have found him.

They dragged him away and placed him in a cell at the local police station.

The Baranoski family were taken away and thrown into a carriage that would take them to Auschwitz. None of them survived the ordeal.

Tadeusz sat on the concrete floor contemplating what his life would be back in Auschwitz. He needn't have worried the following day he was marched out into a courtyard where he faced six SS soldiers. The order was given and the first person to escape from Auschwitz slumped to the ground. They threw his bullet-riddled body in an unmarked grave at the back of the village.

# THE PENAL COMPANY

## CHAPTER 3

There was only one place worse than Auschwitz and that was The Penal Company Auschwitz.

The penal company was created in early August 1940, originally for Catholic priests and the few Jews who were in Auschwitz at the time. Later, any prisoner could be sent there. The majority were Poles, although there were also Jews, Germans, and, in 1944, Soviet POWs. Prisoners were assigned to the penal company for various reasons, including escape attempts, contact with civilians, the illegal possession of food, money, additional clothing, or family photographs, or sluggishness at work—in the opinion of the SS supervisors. The penal company was housed in block 11 in the main camp

In May 1942, it was moved to Birkenau sector.

Prisoners in the penal company were completely isolated. They were forbidden to contact other prisoners or receive correspondence. They performed the hardest labour, usually at double time or on the run. At the same time, they were liable to be beaten continually by SS men and the Kapos. Assignment to the penal company lasted from one month to one year.


A penal company for women was created in June 1942. These prisoners were first housed near the Buda sub-camp before being moved to Birkenau in the spring of 1943. The women were mostly Polish and Jewish, but there were also some Germans. Their labour included dredging mud and clearing rushes from ponds, digging ditches, demolishing buildings, and building roads. At labour, they were subjected to continual beating. In early October 1942, German women functionary prisoners used clubs and hatchets to kill about 90 prisoners in the penal company—mostly Jewish women from France—under the pretext of suppressing a mutiny. In July 1944, the entire women's penal company was transferred to Ravensbrück Concentration Camp. There, the prisoners were placed in blocks along with other prisoners, in effect freeing them from their punishment.

The Ravensbrück concentration camp was the largest concentration camp for women in the German Reich. In the concentration camp system, Ravensbrück was second in size only to the women's camp in Auschwitz-Birkenau.

The first prisoners interned at Ravensbrück were approximately 900 women whom the SS had transferred from the Lichtenburg women's concentration camp in Saxony in May 1939. By the end of 1942, the female inmate population of Ravensbrück had grown to about 10,000. In January 1945, the camp had more than 50,000 prisoners, mostly women.

One of the cruellest sadistic guards at Ravensbrück was Irma Grese. She was born on October 7, 1923 in Germany. She left school at the age of 15 and began her SS career at the age of 19 having been a nurse for 2 years.

In 1943 she was transferred to Auschwitz and was soon promoted to Senior SS-Supervisor in charge of approximately 30,000 women prisoners predominately Polish and Jews.

This was the second highest rank that a female SS officer could attain.

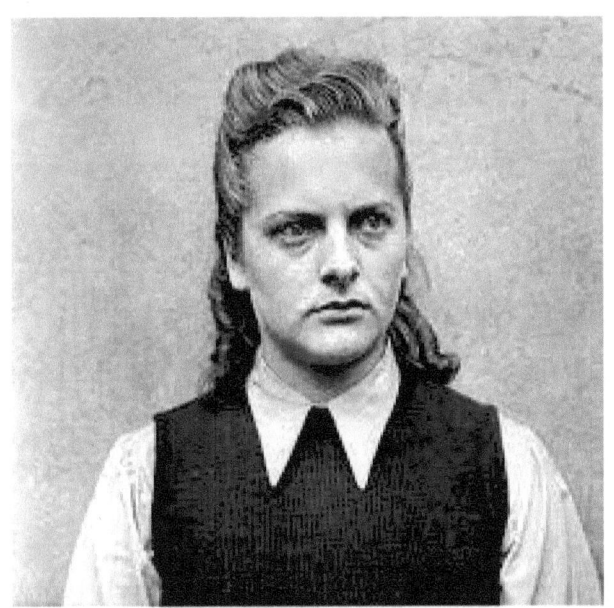

**Irma Grese**

The female prisoners were assembled outside their barracks a roll call was called and to their relief all prisoners were accounted for. If a prisoner were missing there would be hell to pay.

**Irma the Hyena at roll call**

Irma didn't need an excuse to beat an inmate to death she did it for the shear pleasure of watching a Jewish whore die.

Prisoner number 3429 seemed to be marching slowly to the work place in Irma's opinion she pulled her out of the marching group and proceeded to whip her until she took her last breath.

'You two take this scum to the crematorium and come back and join the work detail. Don't be too long or I'll whip you both to death. I might anyway.'

Irma liked to kill prisoners in all different ways it amused her greatly.

'Greta do you think I could kill two Jews with a single bullet?'

'No, I think that would be impossible even for you Irma.'

'Come with me and I'll show you.'

The two SS guards left their quarters and began their search for suitable victims.

Irma spotted two sisters they would be ideal.

'You two come here, the shorter of you stand in front of me now the taller stand behind facing the same way. Excellent now open your mouth.'

Irma removed her Luger from its holster stuck it in the first sister's mouth and pulled the trigger. Both girls were killed instantly.

'So, what do you think Greta I told you I could kill two with a single bullet.'

'I'm glad I didn't put a wager on it Irma.'

'What should we do with these two?'

'Just leave them somebody will clean up the mess.'

The two women walked back to their quarters laughing as they went.

The inmates that witnessed the atrocity just walked away they were used to German cruelty.

**The two sisters before Auschwitz**

Auschwitz was multi cultural.

The inmates came from over 30 countries. The greatest numbers came from Poland (36%), Soviet Union (21%), the German Reich (18%, includes Austria), Hungary (8%), France (6%), Czechoslovakia (3%), the Benelux countries (2%), and Yugoslavia (2%).

# Life in the Penal Company

The convicts were assigned to the hardest work. It was backbreaking labour, insulting all human dignity. Additionally, Germans systematically executed many detainees. In such a situation, the Auschwitz prisoners, among whom a large group were members of an underground network established in the camp by Captain Witold Pilecki, decided to escape. They developed a plan: the escape was to take place on June 10 after the signal announced the end of the work on digging a drainage ditch in Birkenau and returning to the camp.

Due to a terrible misunderstanding, the escape was only partially successful. As a result of heavy rain, the head of the penal company, SS officer Otto Moll, announced the end of work earlier. The whistle confused the prisoners and, consequently, around 50 of them began to run away. The Germans opened fire killing 13 prisoners immediately. Thereafter, Kapos turned a dozen back. Two were arrested in the chase and later placed in the bunker of Block 11. However, nine Poles managed to escape. These brave individuals won back their freedom: Józef Traczyk, August Kowalczyk, Eugeniusz Stoczewski, Jerzy Łachecki, Tadeusz Chróścicki junior, Zenon Piernikowski, Jan Laskowski, Józef Pamrow, and Aleksander Buczyński.

Those who weren't so lucky were herded to the Auschwitz concentration camp. The next day the Germans shot 20 prisoners and killed 320 from the penal company in the gas chamber.

# PRISONER BY CHOICE

## CHAPTER 4

## Witold Pilecki

Who was Witold Pilecki and why was he interned in Auschwitz?

**THE TWO FACES OF WITOLD PILECKI**

Witold Pilecki was born in a small village in Russia in 1901 his parents were devout Catholics they were descendants of a noble and wealthy family. The family of seven had been deported from Lithuania to Russia for taking part in an uprising against the government. The family's estate was largely confiscated requiring Witold's father, Julian, to earn a living as a forestry inspector.

Witold was a bright student he excelled in both his primary years and his secondary schooling.

In 1910 Witold moved with his mother and four siblings to Vilnius the once capital of Lithuania to attend school while Julian remained back in his village, Olonets.

**Olonets**

Witold joined the Polish Scouting and Guiding Association.

He established a new branch when he was sent to school in Oryol, which was regarded as a safe haven as WWI had broken out.

He felt compelled to return to Wilno in 1918 as the Russian Revolution had occurred as well as the defeat of Germany and her allies. Understandably he had the desire to live in Poland once more.

He joined a paramilitary force under Major General Wladyslaw Wejtko Their mandate was to disarm German troops and defend the city from a possible attack from the Russians.

The possibility turned into reality when Wilno fell to Bolshevik forces on January 5 1919. Pilecki and his unit resorted to partisan warfare behind Russian lines. Eventually, he and some of his comrades retreated to Bialystok and enlisted in Poland's volunteer army.

Pilecki participated in several conflicts including the Polish-Soviet War.

## Between Two Wars

In 1921 Pilecki was promoted to the rank of corporal. In 1925 he was promoted to the rank of ensign. He was commissioned to the rank of second Lieutenant the following year.

Also in 1926, he inherited the family's estate of Sukurcze.

**Sukurcze Homestead**

Pilecki married his sweetheart Maria Ostrowska they had two children in the first two years of their marriage.

As a result of the tensions between Poland and Germany Pilecki was elevated to the rank of cavalry platoon commander.

As expected Germany invaded Poland the Poles including Pilecki fought hard against the aggressors. The Russians also invaded Poland, which almost completely destroyed the Polish forces.

The remnants of the Polish army retreated to France only a few stayed on to create an underground movement. One of those who stayed on to fight was Pilecki.

**Polish Underground Soldiers**

**Polish Underground Insignia**

# August 1940

**Polish Political Prisoners Arriving at Auschwitz**

Political prisoners were imprisoned in Auschwitz in 1940 it wasn't long before their families were informed of their deaths.

'What do we know about this place Auschwitz Witold?' Asked the officer in charge of the underground group.

'To be honest General we don't know much about it except it is a prison camp for political prisoners from several country's including Germany.'

General Michael Tokarzewski was the senior officer in charge of the underground movement appointed by Marshal Eduard Rydz- Smigly, the Commander-in-Chief of the Polish Army.

'I think we need to find out what's going on behind those electric fences.' Said the General.

'Does anybody here have a suggestion?'

'I have a suggestion General.'

'Well, what is it Pilecki?'

'I will get myself arrested and get transported to Auschwitz.'

'Are you sure you want to do that Pilecki you may never return?'

'Sir our soldiers are putting themselves on the line daily. A ferocious enemy is killing many. I am more than willing to determine what is happening to our citizens in Auschwitz.'

'I admire your courage Pilecki.'

'I will see you when this horrible war is over General.'

'I hope so son I really do.'

## September 19 1940

The Germans were conducting street roundups in Warsaw, Pilecki ensured he was arrested.

**Pilecki being loaded on a Truck**

Pilecki was detained along with 1800 Polish political prisoners in a camp on the outskirts of Warsaw for a few days and then transported by rail to Auschwitz.

**Auschwitz**

Auschwitz remained Pilecki's home for the next two and a half years.

His mission was to raise the morale of his fellow Polish prisoners.

Nothing could have prepared him for the brutality he found. As he leapt out of a train car with hundreds of other men, he was beaten with clubs. Ten men were randomly pulled from the group and shot. Another man was asked about his profession; when he said he was a doctor, he was beaten to death. Anyone who was educated or Jewish was beaten. Those remaining were robbed of their valuables, stripped, shaved, assigned a number and prison stripes, and then marched out to stand in the first of many roll calls.

'Attention, let none of you imagine that you will ever leave this place alive' shouted Stefan Baretzki.

'The rations have been calculated so that you will only survive for six weeks.'

Stefan Baretzki was an Auschwitz guard of Bukovina German origin. He was conscripted into the Waffen-SS and stationed at the Auschwitz concentration camp from 1942 until 1945. There he participated in the mass murder by making selections, beatings and murdering prisoners on his own initiative.

Stefan Baretzki is on the far right of this photo. His cane in hand was used to beat the new arrivals at Auschwitz.

**Pilecki's First Roll Call**

When Pilecki arrived at the camp there were no gas chambers however the crematoriums were running full tilt. A common saying by the guards was 'the only was out of Auschwitz was through the chimney.'

The new arrivals were assigned tattoos on the outer side of their left forearm.

Pilecki's number was 4859 over 400.000 tattoos were given to prisoners.

Witold and his inmates, 500 in all were squeezed into their barracks, number 32.

He observed the basic accommodation it was dark due to the fact it lacked windows.

The 36 bunk beds were meant to hold 300 prisoners however the number was closer to 500. There was one benefit being so close and personal provided some warmth. There was no insulation and the average October evening temperature was 4 degrees.

Witold found a spot on the bunk bed to lie down. It wasn't long before he felt his stomach stirring and rumbling. He got up quickly and raced to the toilet he knew the signs of diarrhoea. The toilet was a bucket at the end of the hut. He was required to squat over the bucket in front of his fellow inmates.

This was not a pleasant experience for him or his fellow prisoners.

It wasn't long before Witold gathered a small group of Polish underground colleagues to form the "Military Organisation Union" (ZOW) to smuggle food into the camp and smuggle out detailed reports of genocide to the West. Apart from his clandestine activities Pilecki number 4859 was forced to break and wheelbarrow large rocks.

'Witold I have been approached by a Jewish electrical engineer with a stunning proposal.'

'I wouldn't have thought there was much need for an electrical engineer in this place Kacper.'

'Well, I think there is he assures me he can build a radio transmitter allowing us to communicate with the out side world.'

'How's he going to obtain the parts?'

'He assures me he can get them apparently he already has most of what he needs.'

'You're sure you can trust him?'

"Witold he's fucking Jewish no way will he betray us he hates the Germans more than we do.'

'I'll run it past the other members of ZOW, I'm sure they will approve the plan.'

'They will if you endorse it.'

ZOW endorsed the plan with enthusiasm Pilecki began his secret transmissions to the British High Command. Initially, he reported the atrocious conditions the POWs were forced to live in.

His reports changed in September 1941 when trainloads of Jews and other ethnic groups such as Russians were arriving on mass and being gassed upon arrival at Auschwitz.

The allies did not believe the reports no country would do such a thing.

While in Auschwitz, Pilecki became the leader of ZOW. They did what they could to keep up morale, steal food and medicine for those in dire need, and continue to send out information to the Allies.

To fight back, they harvested lice infected with typhoid and put them on the uniforms of the most sadistic guards. Many of them died as a result. Prisoners were kept busy working on expanding Auschwitz, not realizing what it was for.

## The Escape

With no help forthcoming from the Allies, Pilecki and two others broke out of Auschwitz on the evening of April 26, 1943.

They successfully removed the bolts from a heavy door whilst the guards' backs were turned. The three escapees journeyed for 100km on foot before they could rest in relative safety. It took them a week.

Pilecki took refuge at a friend's parents' home before visiting the nearest member of the Polish resistance movement, the Home Army. After three and a half months, and still, no action taken by the Home Army to liberate Auschwitz, Pilecki returned to Warsaw totally frustrated.

Ever the patriot he fought in the Warsaw Uprising of 1944 but their defeat led to Pilecki's imprisonment by the Germans once again

When the camps were liberated at the end of the war, Pilecki was sent to Italy where he joined the Polish Armed Forces. It was here where he wrote his comprehensive report on his time in Auschwitz, which became known as "Witold's Report". Despite his relative safety in Italy, Pilecki returned once again to Warsaw to gather intelligence on the newly established Polish Communist government. The Nazis had been overthrown, but so had the Polish Government-in-exile. To Pilecki and the Home Army, Poland was still not free, but subservient to their Soviet liberators.

The Communist Polish authorities captured Pilecki on 8 May 1947. Accused of spying and of planning to assassinate key figures in the Polish police, he was coerced and tortured to sign his 'confession'.

Pilecki stood an unfair trial where he was not permitted to testify, nor were there any defending witnesses. The trial was a sham – a deterrent to any other would-be opposition to the Communist regime. He was subsequently found guilty and executed on 25 May 1948 in Mokotow prison with a shot to the back of his head.

In 1990, shortly after the collapse of the Soviet Union and the Communist regime in Poland, Pilecki was finally exonerated posthumously and recognised for his actions during World War Two.

# KNOWLEDGE WILL SAVE LIVES

## CHAPTER 5

Rudolf Vrba was born on 11 September 1924 in Slovakia (now the Czech Republic).

In 1942 he became aware that the Germans were rounding up all the Jews and transporting them to God knows where.

'I don't like what's happening around here I'm sure it's not what the Germans are telling us about shipping everybody to a safe haven, I don't trust the bastards.' Said, Rudolf.

'So what can you do Rudolf?' asked his friend Henrich.

'Get out of here quick and head for England where Jews can live safely.'

'What if you get caught they will shoot you.'

'They will shoot me regardless Henrich they're Nazis.'

'I'm not going to risk it Rudolf but I wish you God's speed my friend.'

'Thanks Henrich, I hope you survive in this uncertain world and we meet again on the other side of this terrible war.'

Rudolf packed a backpack with the essentials one change of clothing a cheese roll and a loaf of bread. He also packed a bottle of water.

His mother although not wanting her son to leave on such a perilous journey gave him 200 Crowns a significant amount.

Rudolf knew he could not travel to Sered near the Hungarian border by train as the Germans checked every passenger. Walking was out of the question so he decided to take a taxi. The taxi driver though not a Jew was a family friend.

Rudolf realised the irony of making his escape by taxi however it was the safest mode of transport available to him.

The taxi driver who agreed to the perilous journey was aware of the risk they were both taking.

The taxi arrived in Sered at 5.30 am Rudolf paid the driver 100 shillings and thanked him.

The hardest part of the first day of his escape was about to begin he began the trek to Galanta in Hungry.

It was snowing heavily when Rudolf headed off for Galanta he trudged through the snow for hours it was more than once he thought of turning around and heading back to his warm home and the arms of his mother.

Finally, he saw the dim lights of Galanta. He had made it to Hungry the first part of his journey was nearly over.

A school friend, Stefan, had an aunty in the town he assured Rudolf she would give him refuge for a few days.

Rudolf walked through the town carefully avoiding any police who might be patrolling.

At last, he found the house and knocked on the imposing front door.

He knocked loudly, a maid opened the door took a look at Rudolf and slammed it back in his face.

Rudolf was stunned; he knocked again this time a distinguished woman answered.

'Who are you and what do you want?'

'I am Stefan's friend he suggested you would give me lodgings for a short while.'

'You're Stefan's friend? How do you know my nephew?'

'We went to school together.'

'You better come in then.'

Rudolf was a little shell-shocked - he expected a warmer welcome than he received.

As he was being led down the hall of the magnificent house he saw his reflection in a long mirror.

What he saw was a filthy bedraggled youth who was covered in mud his eyes were bloodshot and his hair was tangled.

'I think you better have a bath young man. Tell me how did you become so filthy?'

'I walked from Sered over fields to ensure I wasn't detected'

'Are you telling me you are here illegally?'

'Yes madam, I intend to reach England.'

'Oh my dear God. Take a bath then we can talk at breakfast.' She returned downstairs shaking her head as she went.

Rudolf had never had such a luxurious bath, yes; the bathroom was beautiful but the deep bath full of warm water felt magnificent. He reluctantly climbed out after half an hour.

His clothes had been cleaned and pressed, and he felt like a new man.

Rudolf went downstairs to join the family for breakfast. The woman's husband a very distinctive man had joined us.

'Welcome to our table boy, what is your name?'

'Rudolf sir.'

'I believe you are a close friend of our nephew Stefan?'

'Yes sir we went to high school together.'

'Excellent well eat up I imagine you have acquired quite an appetite.'

Once breakfast had been consumed the interrogation began.

'Do you have any understanding what life is like now in Hungry?' asked Wilhelm.

'No not really sir. I imagine better than Slovakia.

'We are under martial law. Not only that our relationship with Slovakia is so damaged that any body from Slovakia caught in Hungry will be jailed immediately. Anybody harbouring a Slovakian will be jailed as a spy.'

'Then I must leave this house my presence is putting you in danger.'

'Yes you yourself are in great danger but we need to organise your departure carefully. In the meantime sit tight here and don't venture outside.'

Second-class train tickets to Budapest were purchased and Rudolf began his trip to the nation's capital.

Once he reached Budapest Rudolf headed for the OMZsA a Zionist organisation whose address was given to him by a friend. His objective was to see if they would help him escape.

Instead, he was beaten and kicked out of the building.

They dragged the young Rudolf out past the city limits and threw him down onto the snow.

'We can't shoot the bastard it will draw attention from the Hungarian Patrol.'

'No best we bayonet him instead. The Hungarian Police halted the execution and Rudolf was once again dragged to the Police Station.

From there he was held in the Novaky Detention Camp in Slovakia. He was determined to escape however his determination did not pay dividends he was caught.

He was sent to Auschwitz on June 30 1942. As the scared passengers were assembled on the platform SS divided them into two groups those that were told they needed to shower and those who were selected to work. Rudolf was one of those selected to work, 90% of the people were marched off to the shower block, which turned out to be the gas chamber.

**The Gas Chamber has completed its work**

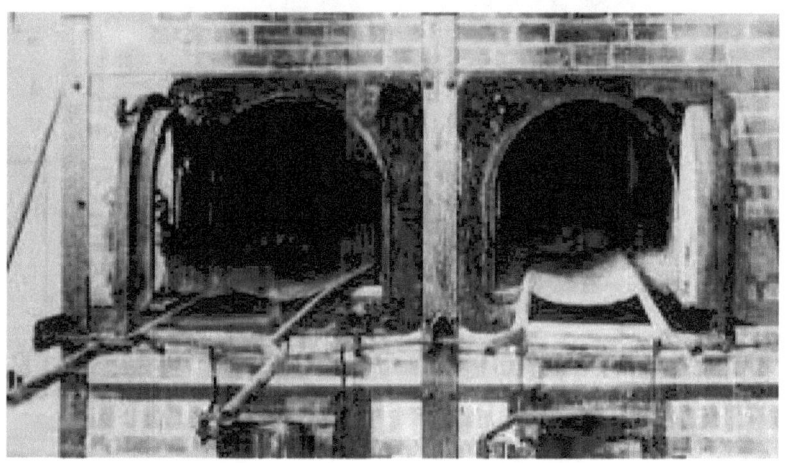

**Crematorium Up to 6 bodies at a time**

Rudolf's work encompassed cleaning up the train wagons of dead bodies additionally he was required to sort through the personal possessions that the victims had been instructed to leave behind while they showered. They were all assured their possessions would be returned to them.

Rudolf's work convinced him the only way the Germans could conduct murder on an industrial scale was to hide the fact as to where the prisoners were going and for what purpose.

He knew the only way he could save the remaining Jews in Europe was to inform them what was happening.

This knowledge would encourage resistance and hinder the German slaughter.

Rudolf was transferred to a desk job, a much more pleasant role which also gave him critical information. He gathered statistics on how many train arrived at Auschwitz and how many arrivals were murdered.

In early 1944 he learnt that the Nazis were preparing for arrival of Hungary's entire Jewish population of around one million people, who were to be exterminated. Vrba had considered attempting escape from Auschwitz before, but now he saw that it was urgent. He felt the members of the organised resistance movement in Auschwitz were focused on their own survival, and not on provoking resistance from the people who arrived to be gassed.

Together with his friend Alfréd Wetzlerthey he analysed previous unsuccessful escape attempts. Using this information they believed they could learn from the mistakes made and escape from Auschwitz. Every day some prisoners would work outside the main camp fence, within an outer perimeter. Vrba and Wetzler scammed their way into the work detail they hid in a pile of wood, which they surrounded by strong-smelling petrol-soaked Russian tobacco, which they had discovered would deter sniffer dogs. When the Nazis discovered Vrba and Wetzler had failed to return to the camp they spent three days searching the area between the inner and outer perimeter. The search ended after the third day, and on the evening of 10 April 1944 Vrba and Wetzler escaped Auschwitz and began an eleven-night trek south to Slovakia, 80 miles away.

After crossing the border into Slovakia the pair quickly made contact with the local Jewish Council. They were interviewed separately to ensure their accounts could be verified. A report was then written and rewritten, and translated into German and Hungarian, becoming a 40-page document.

The report contained descriptions of the camp, including detailed descriptions of the gas chambers at Birkenau and the process of extermination. Much of the report was devoted to painstakingly remembered details of the transports, which had arrived at Auschwitz – including the nationalities and numbers of those who arrived and died.

The motivating factor behind the escape was not only freedom but to save many more Jews particularly Hungarian from the murderous hands of the Germans.

The Vrba-Wetzler's Report was largely ignored by the leaders of the Hungarian community on the basis they were negotiating with the Germans to save some of the Jewish community.

Their inaction resulted in 470,000 Jews being gassed at Auschwitz between 15 May and 7 July 1944.

Eleven months later the Germans surrendered.

Back in Slovakia the 19-year-old Walter Rosenberg was protected by the local Jewish authorities, and given identity papers for 'Rudolf Vrba' – the name he adopted for the rest of his life. Vrba joined the Czechoslovak partisans and fought bravely.

After the war he studied biology and chemistry in Prague. He married his childhood sweetheart, Gerta, though the relationship did not last long. Vrba escaped communist Czechoslovakia by defecting whilst on a visit to a scientific conference in Israel. He left Israel after a couple of years, as he was not comfortable living among some of the leaders of the Hungarian Jewish community who he blamed for failing to raise awareness of the mass killings at Auschwitz. He moved to Britain, and then to Canada, where he remarried.

The Vrba–Wetzler Report was a significant piece of evidence at the Nuremberg war crimes trials in 1946. Vrba sent evidence to the trial of Adolf Eichmann in Jerusalem in 1961, and was a witness at a trial of Holocaust denier Ernst Zündel in Toronto in 1985. He died in 2006.

**Rudolf Vrba Died: 27 March 2006 aged 81**

# SOBIBOR

## CHAPTER 6

## March 1942

Sobibor was the third extermination camp to be established by the Germans. The site was chosen because of its remoteness and the fact it was connected to the railway network.

Initially, only 700 Jewish workers resided there; they were used for forced labour to extend the original camp's facilities.

This number grew dramatically as more and more Jews arrived by train.

Sobibor consisted of two camps, which were divided into three sections.

1. Administration
2. Barracks
3. Storage

The final extension comprised the extermination centre.

Three gas chambers (Carbon monoxide)

An additional three gas chambers were added later.

Crematoriums

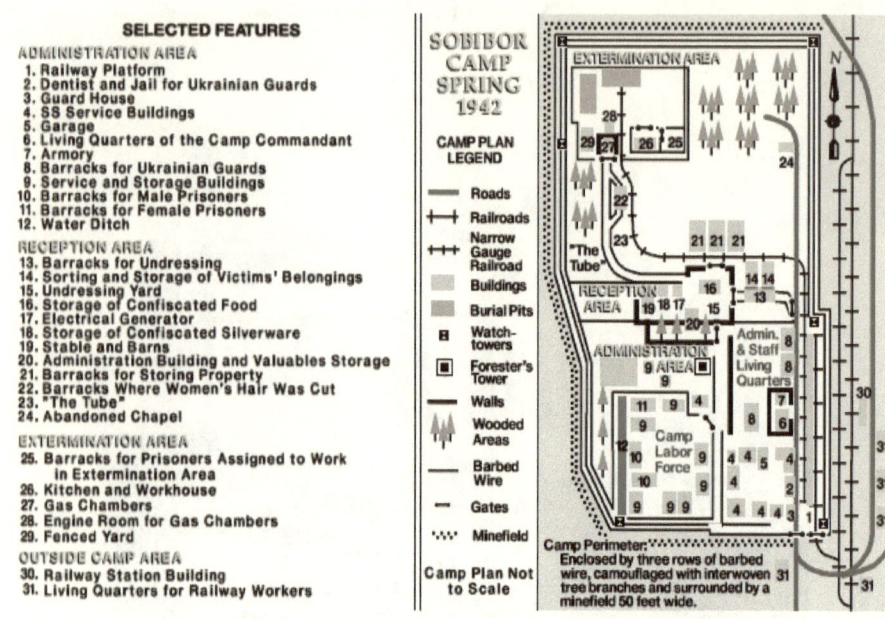

**SELECTED FEATURES**

**ADMINISTRATION AREA**
1. Railway Platform
2. Dentist and Jail for Ukrainian Guards
3. Guard House
4. SS Service Buildings
5. Garage
6. Living Quarters of the Camp Commandant
7. Armory
8. Barracks for Ukrainian Guards
9. Service and Storage Buildings
10. Barracks for Male Prisoners
11. Barracks for Female Prisoners
12. Water Ditch

**RECEPTION AREA**
13. Barracks for Undressing
14. Sorting and Storage of Victims' Belongings
15. Undressing Yard
16. Storage of Confiscated Food
17. Electrical Generator
18. Storage of Confiscated Silverware
19. Stable and Barns
20. Administration Building and Valuables Storage
21. Barracks for Storing Property
22. Barracks Where Women's Hair Was Cut
23. "The Tube"
24. Abandoned Chapel

**EXTERMINATION AREA**
25. Barracks for Prisoners Assigned to Work in Extermination Area
26. Kitchen and Workhouse
27. Gas Chambers
28. Engine Room for Gas Chambers
29. Fenced Yard

**OUTSIDE CAMP AREA**
30. Railway Station Building
31. Living Quarters for Railway Workers

**SOBIBOR CAMP SPRING 1942**

**CAMP PLAN LEGEND**

- Roads
- Railroads
- Narrow Gauge Railroad
- Buildings
- Burial Pits
- Watch-towers
- Forester's Tower
- Walls
- Wooded Areas
- Barbed Wire
- Gates
- Minefield

Camp Plan Not to Scale

Camp Perimeter: Enclosed by three rows of barbed wire, camouflaged with interwoven tree branches and surrounded by a minefield 50 feet wide.

The death camp measured approximately 1,300 by 2000 feet it was surrounded by a triple line of barbed wire and watchtowers were strategically placed.

The camp was small compared to other camps.

Twenty railway wagons could be accommodated on the platforms.

The Jews and other prisoners were taken from the train and instructed to undress ready to shower. They had their haircut and then led into the gas chamber.

**Leon Feldhendler**

Leon was the head of the Jewish Council in his village Żółkiewka, Lublin Voivodeship in German-occupied Poland.

Leon along with the remainder of the Jews in the village was rounded up and loaded onto cattle wagons heading for Sobibor.

'Where do you think they are taking us Leon?' asked his young cousin Ludwick.

'I don't know son but I have a feeling we're not going to a holiday camp.'

Leon was fortunate he had a cousin already in the camp. Leon's cousin convinced a German officer that Leon was a skilled carpenter. The rest of the family were not so fortunate, they were all gassed.

When the prisoners were locked away at night they could converse amongst themselves freely without the guards hearing them.

Leon became the ringleader he developed a plan to escape.

'The only was we can get out of this place is to escape.' Said Leon.

'Easier said than done.' Said Philip.

'There's no denying it will be difficult but unless you want to leave here in a puff of smoke I suggest we devise a plan.' Said Leon.

'I have secured some vials of arsenic; don't ask me how I obtained it. We should poison some guards and steal their weapons' said Leon.

'It sounds like a long shot but what else have we got?' said Tomasz.

Unfortunately, the Germans uncovered the plan. They chose five prisoners and led them out to the parade ground and shot them while the other prisoners were forced to watch.

Another plan considered was to set fire to the camp creating mass confusion. The Germans had laid land mines around the camp perimeter making the plan impractical.

# Leon Pechersky

Leon Pechersky was born in Kremenchuk, Ukraine, in 1909; Pechersky came from a respected Jewish family. During the First World War, his family moved to Rostov-on-Don. Surviving the Russian Civil War, which was especially brutal in Ukraine.

On June 22, 1941, the opening day of Operation Barbarossa. Pechersky's life changed forever. He was conscripted along with thousands of young Russian men. He was posted to the 596th Howitzer Regiment part of the Soviet 19th Army. He along with his comrades experienced the horror of Belorussia one of the darkest days of the German invasion.

Altogether, more than 2 million people were killed in Belarus during the three years of Nazi occupation, almost a quarter of the region's population, including 500,000 to 550,000 Jews.

He was quickly promoted to the technical quartermaster, essentially the rank of a 1st lieutenant. When the 19th Army tried to stem the Wehrmacht's advance to Moscow in October, Pechersky's unit was encircled and he was captured.

The rumours he had heard regarding the brutality of the Germans proved to be true.

He was sent to a site near Minsk in Belorussia. Pechersky was able to conceal his Jewishness. Life was far from easy apart from the brutality meted out by the sadistic guards he contracted typhus. Despite not receiving any medical treatment he survived.

Peckershy's toughness and good fortune would serve him well. In May 1943, after an escape attempt, German officials transferred him from Borisov to Stalag 352, one of the most atrocious prison camps of World War II. Up to 80,000 soldiers from the Red Army died in this camp at Minsk between July 1941 and August 1943. Held in the so-called Waldlager (forest camp), in the nearby village of Masyukovchina, Pechersky's luck appeared to have run out that August when a German investigation of men who had been circumcised led to the discovery of his Jewish identity. Camp officials promptly shut Pechersky into an underground cell before removing him to the part of Stalag 352 set up in Minsk itself. The Germans kept him there until September 18.

That day, a train packed with 2000 people, many of them Soviet soldiers, brought Pechersky into Sobibor. Thankfully, the Nazis committed a gigantic blunder right away, one that would come to haunt them. They selected about 80 of the soldiers to be spared immediate death. Instead, they would do labour. Pechersky was one of them. He convinced the SS on his arrival that he was a carpenter. This lie saved his life.

The norm was 80% gassed and the remainder would be put to hard labour. Many of these workers died in the first year.

It didn't take long for Pechersky to be appointed as the escape ringleader with Feldhendler as his deputy.

It only took three weeks for Pechersky and his escape group to work out a detailed plan.

The plan relied on the experienced Soviet POWs to kill some of the SS guards taking their rifles and uniforms.

Each evening the 600 prisoners would assemble for roll call, the Soviets dressed in their SS uniforms would shoot the guards manning the gate and guard tower. The prisoners would then flee through the gate.

Pechersky learnt that the camp commandant and his senior officers had been called to a meeting outside the camp.

This would be the ideal opportunity to instigate the breakout.

## October 14 1943

The uprising began at 4 pm. The prisoners who worked as tailors invited the deputy commandant into the tailor's shop so that he could be fitted for a new suit. As he stepped inside he was killed with an axe.

The same ploy was conducted in Camp Two the prisoners suggested to SS officer Josef Wulf to try on a victim's overcoat. He too was killed with an axe.

Over the next hour nine more guards were disposed of in a similar manner.

At 5 pm the prisoners gathered as usual, the SS guards realised some of their number were missing. They opened fire on the prisoners however, they did not expect the return fire from the escape group who had stolen the German weapons. Over 300 prisoners escaped from the camp.

The Germans shot many of the escaping prisoners others died from exploding land mines, which surrounded the camp.

A massive manhunt was organised over the next few days resulting in over 100 prisoners being shot.

It was estimated 200 prisoners escaped unharmed however only 50 survived the war. German villagers and Polish civilians betrayed the remainder.

**Sobibor Survivors**

**Sobibor Survivors**

One couple that remained free and went on to live a peaceful life after the war was Chaim Engel and Selma.

Both Chaim and Selma were lucky they were not chosen to be gassed rather they had been selected to work in the clothing-sorting hut. Their jobs were to select clothes that could be worn by poor German families.

**Sorting Victims Clothing**

Chaim could not stop looking at the beautiful girl opposite him in the sorting shed. He contrived all sorts of reasons to talk to her. Usually it was asking her if a particular piece of woman's underwear was worth keeping. He needed to be careful if the guards decided it was frivolous chit chat they would both be beaten.

Despite the restrictions over time they fell in love, when the guards weren't looking they would hold hands or just look at each other with love in their eyes.

It was Selma that stole a knife for Chaim to kill a SS guard during the uprising.

The couple were able to escape in the uprising they found refuge with Polish farmers there they remained in their barn for nine months at last the Germans retreated from Poland in July 1944. Selma became pregnant with their first child.

The couple married and travelled through Eastern Europe and then boarded a ship to Marseille in France.

Their son, Emiel tragically died on route. From France they travelled to Selma's home country, the Netherlands where they lived with Selma's parents in their hotel.

Two more children were born they then immigrated to Israel however Selma did not feel safe there so the decision was made to immigrate to America.

Chaim died in Bradford Connecticut in 2003. Selma died in 2018 aged 96.

# AUDACIOUS ESCAPE

## CHAPTER 7

**Maidanek Camp**

**Lublin**

**July 14 1942**

Lublin is the capital of Lubelskie in Poland.

Its history dates back to the 9th century when a large castle was built and the town grew up around it. The town grew and reached its economic peak in the 16th century.

Through the events of various wars in Europe it passed to Austria in 1795 and then Russia in 1815.

The Germans established Majdanek concentration camp on the outskirts of Lublin during WW2.

**Majdanek Camp**

Soviet POWs were the first to be incarcerated in the camp it was these men who built the camp under German supervision.

They were subjected to extremely brutal treatment, which resulted in very high mortality rate. Out of the first Soviet deportees brought to Majdanek in October 1941, nearly 95% died by the end of the year.

They died from beatings, malnutrition and various diseases.

In early 1942 the majority of the POWs decided the only way to survive was to escape.

# July 14 1942

When night fell 86 Soviet prisoners left their barracks and congregated at the southern section of the camp.

At an agreed time the POWs started to throw logs, loose boards from their barracks and blankets onto the barbed wire fence enabling them to climb over and run for their lives.

An unexpected surprise was there were only two guards on duty and they were astonished at what was happening. They didn't shoot at the escapees until it was too late.

Only two POWs were shot and killed by the guards.

The remaining 82 prisoners headed for the village of Kalinowka they hid in the surrounding grain fields and then entered a nearby forest.

A massive manhunt took place over the next few days but to no avail. The Soviets were free.

In the mean time the commandant Karl Otto Koch ordered a roll call on the morning after the breakout.

The count was 41 Soviet POWs. These Soviets had possibly been left out of the plan or they decided they were safer staying in the camp.

The remaining Soviet POWs were all sentenced to death with immediate effect. They were all executed on July 15, early in the morning. They were forced to lay themselves on the ground in several rows, and the SS-man shot them all in the back of their heads. The corpses were then taken to the camp crematorium, the execution site was covered with sawdust. Such was the tragic end of the first prisoners of Majdanek.

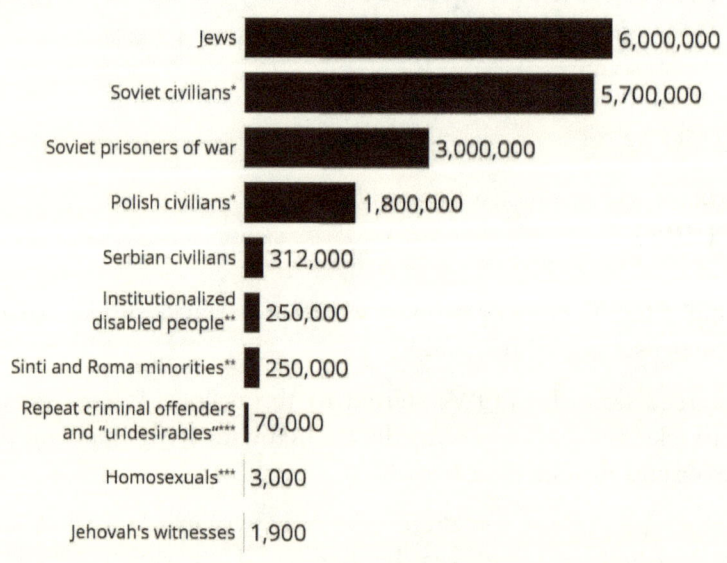

## 17 Million Fell Victim to the Nazi Regime

Estimated number of victims killed by the German Nazi regime and its collaborators (1933-1945)

| | |
|---|---|
| Jews | 6,000,000 |
| Soviet civilians* | 5,700,000 |
| Soviet prisoners of war | 3,000,000 |
| Polish civilians* | 1,800,000 |
| Serbian civilians | 312,000 |
| Institutionalized disabled people** | 250,000 |
| Sinti and Roma minorities** | 250,000 |
| Repeat criminal offenders and "undesirables"*** | 70,000 |
| Homosexuals*** | 3,000 |
| Jehovah's witnesses | 1,900 |

* non-jewish   ** upper estimate   *** lower estimate
Sources: United States Holocaust Memorial Museum, Dr. Alexander Zinn

# JAPAN

**The fruits of victory are tumbling into our mouths too quickly.**

*Emperor Hirohito of Japan, April 29, 1942*

# JAPANESE HOSPITALITY

## CHAPTER 8

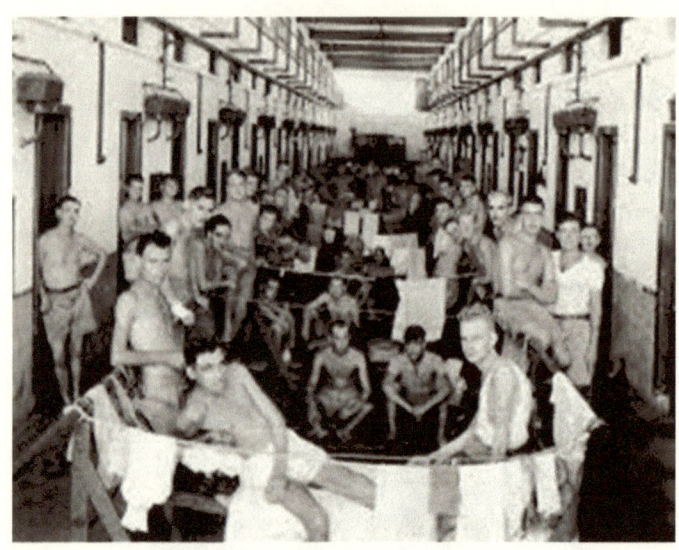

**A Section of Changi Prison**

It was difficult to escape from Japanese camps most of the POWs were Caucasian and therefore stood out from the Asian population.

Changi was one of the more notorious Japanese prisoner of war camps. It was used to imprison Malayan civilians and Allied soldiers. The treatment of POWs at Changi was harsh but fitted in with the belief held by the Japanese Imperial Army that those who had surrendered to it were guilty of dishonouring their country and family and as such deserved to be treated in no other way.

For this reason, forty thousand men from the surrender of Singapore were marched to the northern tip of the island where they were imprisoned at a military base called Selerang, near the village of Changi. The British civilian population of Singapore was imprisoned in Changi Prison itself, one mile away from Selerang. Eventually, any reference to the area was simply made as 'Changi'.

For the first few months the POWs at Changi were allowed to do as they wished with little interference from the Japanese. There was just enough food and medicine provided and to begin with the Japanese seemed indifferent to what the POWs did. Concerts were organised, as were quizzes and sporting events. The camp was organised by the officers into battalions and regiments and strong military discipline was maintained. However, by Easter 1942, the attitude of the Japanese had changed. They organised work parties to repair the damaged docks in Singapore and food and medicine became scarce. More significantly, the Japanese made it clear that they had not signed the Geneva Convention and that they ran the camp based on their own rules.

As 1942 moved on, deaths from dysentery and vitamin deficiencies increased dramatically.

## Escape from Changi

In May 1942, two members of the Royal Australian Army Ordnance Corps, Corporal Rodney Breavington and Private Victor Gale had become prisoners of war under the Japanese in the Fall of Singapore.

'Victor there is not a chance in hell that we will survive living in this hell. The Japs have no respect for human life.'

'I'm more than aware of that sir but escaping is out of the question.'

'Not necessarily I've been thinking the next time we are scheduled to unload a ship we hide somewhere and then pinch a boat and sail off to freedom.'

'With respect sir where do you propose we hide?'

'There is always cargo stacked on the wharf we just need to hide amongst the bales and sneak out at night. There are plenty of boats moored close in we steal one and sail out of the harbour.'

'Surely the Japs will realise they are a couple of POWs short.'

'Probably not they don't call a roll call daily we just need to hope they don't call one that afternoon.'

'Are you suggesting we sail to Australia?'

'No, too bloody far I think it is about 5000 kilometres. I was thinking of Ceylon it's still under British control.'

' How far is that?'

'About 2000 kilometres.'

'What about food and water?'

'If we plan it right we can save some rice and water and hide it on the wharf.'

'Forgive me sir but it sounds like a long shot.'

'Well Victor it's the only shot we've got. Are you with me?'

'OK let's do it after all what have we got to lose?'

Over the next four weeks the Aussie soldiers pilfered as much rice and water as they could. They stole a kerosene burner so that the rice could be boiled.

They found a good hiding place on the wharf. When the work detail were instructed to return to the camp the two escapees were all ready in their hiding spot. The guards were not aware they were two men short the Australians escaped from Singapore in a stolen yacht. It was a marathon effort over about six weeks at sea and 1,900 kilometres. The *Regatta* had adequate water supplies however, barely enough canned food. Their intention was to sail to Ceylon and meet up with British forces.

The two Australians were getting close to their destination when Victor spotted a Royal Navy frigate.

'Rod, I can see a British frigate! We've made it.'

'Fire off one of those flares that should get their attention.'

Sure enough the ship headed in their direction however as the ship got closer they realised it wasn't a British frigate it was a Japanese frigate.

The ship shot several rounds at the Regatta's bow indicating they would be boarded and taken prisoner once again.

The two Australian POWs were manhandled into the ship's brig. It set sail for Singapore.

'I think we might be in a spot of bother mate the Japs don't think kindly of escapees.' Said Rod.

'What do you think will happen to us Rod?'

'Well the usual form of punishment entails a firing squad.'

'Fuck, do you really think they will shoot us?'

'No, I don't think, I know.

'I'll try and save your bacon. I'll say you were just following orders you had no choice but to follow me.'

*The Regatta* **under full sale**

As Breavington faced a firing squad of Sikh Indians who were to shoot then bury him and Gale as well as two British escapees on Selarang Beach, he pleaded unsuccessfully with the Japanese commander to spare 23-year-old Gale.

He then refused a blindfold, opting to hold a photograph of his wife.

The first shot hit him in the arm. He fell to the ground, and then saluted Lieutenant-Colonel Frederick "Black Jack" Galleghan, the most senior Australian soldier present, saying "Goodbye Sir, and good luck".

He was shot eight more times the reason being the Sikhs were terrible shots. All four were buried at Singapore's Kranji War Cemetery.

The attempted escapes enraged the Japanese administration, who demanded that everyone in the camp sign a document declaring that they would not attempt to escape. This was universally refused. As a result, twenty thousand POWs were herded into the Selerang Barracks Square and told that they would remain there until the order was given to sign the document.

The Selerang Barracks, originally built to accommodate eight hundred men, consisted of a parade ground surrounded on three sides by three-storey buildings. A number of smaller houses for officers and married couples were spread out in the spacious grounds. Nearly twenty thousand men crammed into a parade ground of about one hundred and twenty-eight by two hundred and ten metres.

**Selerang Barracks Square**

An Australian POW, George Aspinall documented the situation:

> *The first and most urgent problem we had to face up to was the lack of toilet facilities. Each barracks building had about four to six toilets, which were flushed from small cisterns on the roofs. But the Japanese cut the water off, and these toilets couldn't be used. The Japanese only allowed one water tap to be used, and people used to line up in the early hours of the morning and that queue would go on all day. You were allowed one water bottle of water per man per day, just one quart for your drinking, washing, and everything else. Not that there was much washing done under the circumstances.'*

The few POW doctors were becoming very concerned with the health of the troops and they, along with Lieutenant Colonel 'Weary' Dunlop, knew that if this standoff lasted much longer men were going to die.

'We need to get access to more clean water Lieutenant Colonel. If we don't, they'll start dropping like flies.'

'I know said Bill the senior camp doctor By the way, call me 'Weary'. Everyone else does.'

'Why do they call you Weary?'

'It's my surname - Dunlop. Tyres. Weary.'

'Oh, I get it. Anyway - do you think we could approach the Japanese? See if we can increase the water ration?'

'Bill, we can try. But I think these bastards are going to refuse. Until the assurance of non-escape is signed they're going to squeeze tighter and tighter.'

'Do you reckon we all should sign it and end this fucking stalemate?'

'I do. It's not worth the rice paper it's written on.'

Bill and Weary made a heartfelt plea to the Japanese commander.

'Sir, we beg you to increase the food and water ration to our men. It's causing dysentery and other illnesses. These could spread throughout the entire group.'

'I will increase the ration as soon as your stubborn men sign the document. We have politely asked them to sign. It's up to them.'

Bill and Weary retreated to the barracks knowing that more and more prisoners would die each day they were detained in the unholy square.

After three very hot and humid days and despite the oppressive conditions, the POWs still refused to back down.

General Fukuye ordered the commander of the British and Australian troops in Changi, Lt-Gen E. B. Holmes, and his deputy, Lieutenant Colonel Frederick Galleghan, to attend the execution of the four recent escapees: Breavington, Gale, Waters and Fletcher. One of the Australians, Breavington, pleaded to no avail that he was solely responsible for the escape attempt and should be the only one executed. The Indian National Army guards carried out their executions with rifles on 2nd September. The initial volley was non-fatal, and the wounded men had to plead to be finished off.

This action had no effect on the POWs' position. The Japanese pulled out ten men and marched them to the local beach and shot them all. Despite this, still no one signed the document.

Only when the men were threatened with an epidemic by moving the hospital into the square was the order given that the document should be signed.

Bill and Weary had made it very clear to the officers that moving the sick into the barracks would not only finish off their patients, it would spread disease throughout the ranks – they were already at the end of their tether.

However, having agreed, the commanding officer made it clear that the document was non-binding, as it had been signed under duress. He also knew that his men desperately needed the medicine that the Japanese would have withheld if the document had not been signed. But this episode marked a point of no return for the POWs at Changi.

Bill and his wife Julie had not seen each other since Julie farewelled Bill at Government House that terrible day when the Japanese marched into Singapore. She assumed he was alive although she had heard of the rumours of a massacre at Alexandria Hospital where they both worked. She knew Bill - he would have managed to live somehow.

Being a doctor, Julie was kept busy with looking after the three thousand-odd civilian prisoners at the second Changi Prison, quite close to where Bill was being held.

The civilians were slightly better off than the POWs, with better food rations and water but very little medicine. This made Julie's job all the more difficult.

As in the men's prison, dysentery and malaria were the greatest killers.

Julie was near the perimeter fence hoping to get a glimpse of Bill something she did regularly but without success. This day, she saw two men with a Japanese escort striding over the parade ground heading for the commander's office. She swore it was Bill but couldn't be sure - the man was terribly skinny and wore a hat. She dare not yell out, as she would be beaten severely for unruly behaviour. She waited until the two men returned to the male prison. This time she was sure it was Bill her darling Bill. She now knew for certain that her beloved husband was alive.

The Japanese used the POWs at Changi for slave labour. The formula was very simple; if you worked, you would get fed. If you didn't work, you would starve. Men were made to work in the docks where they loaded munitions onto ships. They were also used to clear sewers damaged in the attack on Singapore. The men who were too ill to work relied on those who could work for their food. Sharing what were already meagre supplies became a way of life – true mateship.

The number of POWs kept at Changi dropped quite markedly as men were constantly shipped out to other areas in the Japanese Empire to work. Men were sent to Borneo or Thailand to work on the Burma-Thai railway or to Japan itself where they were made to work in the mines. More captured soldiers, airmen and sailors from a variety of Allied nations replaced them. Malaria, dysentery and dermatitis were common, as were beatings for not working hard enough.

In 1943, the seven thousand men left at Selerang were moved to the prison in Changi. It was built to hold one thousand. The Japanese crammed five or six men in a cell designed for one. With such overcrowding, disease was rife and spread throughout the prison. The majority of the Red Cross parcels were never distributed; therefore the men at Changi had to rely on their own wits to survive. An example of POW ingenuity was that the army medics made tablets convincing the Japanese guards they were a cure for VD. The tablets became a best seller and they could then buy genuine medicine for their own men in an attempt to aid those who were sick.

As the end of the Pacific War approached, rations to the POWs were reduced and the work requirement increased. POWs were forced to dig tunnels and foxholes in the hills around Singapore, affording the Japanese places to hide and fight when the Allies finally reached Singapore.

Many POWs believed that the Japanese would kill them as the Allies got near to Singapore. This never happened. When Emperor Hirohito told the people of Japan that the war 'has gone not necessarily to our advantage', the Japanese soldiers at Changi simply handed over their weapons and became prisoners themselves.

By the time Changi was liberated over eight thousand Australian POWs had died. The British lost over twelve thousand.

**Accommodation at Changi**

# ESCAPE FROM HONG KONG

## CHAPTER 9

**Sir Mark Young**

## December 8 1941

Sir Mark Young was siting in his office in Government House Hong Kong. Every morning he would read his mail generally there was nothing particularly interesting.

The telephone rang he picked up the receiver slightly annoyed his mail reading had been interrupted.

'Yes?'

'Sir, it's Christopher Maltby I have some very disturbing news.'

'What is it Major General?'

'The Japanese have attacked Pearl Harbour Hawaii.'

'The audacious bastards was there much damage?'

'I don't have the exact toll but all indications are that there has been significant damage to the fleet plus the majority of their planes have been destroyed.'

'I should send a telegram to Washington DC offering our support.'

'I'm sure they will appreciate it although I'm not sure how we will be able to support them.'

'Do we have planes in the air Major General I can hear them overhead.'

'I don't think so Sir I'll go outside and look.'

Major General returned to the phone in his office.

'Sir those planes seem to be Japanese.'

'What do you mean seem either they are or not.'

Just then the first Japanese bombs began to hit their targets.

'No fucking "seems" about it Christopher we are under attack.'

Maltby returned to the Governor's office.

'Sir we are under attack from the Japanese I have no idea how many land troops are involved but if the attack is anything like Manchuria we will be overwhelmed within a short time..'

*The British had 14,000 troops, 5 planes, 4 gunboats and 1 minelayer*

*The Japanese had 27,000 troops, 47 planes, 3 destroyers 4 torpedo boats and 3 gunboats*

**Japanese Bomb Hong Kong**

'As far as I know we are not at war with the Japanese.' Said Mark Aitchison.'

'Well we are now sir they have inflicted significant damage according to garrison head quarters.'

British, Canadian and Indian forces defended Hong Kong. The Hong Kong Volunteer Defence Forces did their best to support them.

The sheer numbers of Japanese troops who were well equipped and well trained unlike the defenders overwhelmed these troops.

The first wave of Japanese troops landed in Hong Kong with artillery fire for cover and the following order from their commander: "Take no prisoners." Upon overrunning a volunteer antiaircraft battery, the Japanese invaders roped together the captured soldiers and proceeded to bayonet them to death. Even those who offered no resistance, such as the Royal Medical Corps, were led up a hill and murdered. This brutality became the norm for Japanese soldiers.

The Japanese quickly took control of key reservoirs, threatening the British and Chinese inhabitants with a slow death by thirst. Initially declining the Japanese commanders invitation to surrender the Governor Mark Aitchison decided it was a lost cause and surrendered to the invaders on Christmas Day 1941.

The surrender papers were signed at the Peninsula Hotel on the 26th of December.

Hong Kong had become a protectorate of Japan for the next four years.

Led by General Rensuke Isogai, the Japanese established their administrative centre and military headquarters at the Peninsula Hotel in Kowloon.

**General Rensuke Isogai**

**Peninsula Hotel Japanese HQ**

The Japanese were concerned Chinese citizens may assist the allies to retake Hong Kong subsequently they deported over one million Hong Kong Chinese to Mainland China.

The Japanese established a number of POW camps including Ma Tau Chung to house Indians who refused to fight alongside the Japanese.

The buildings in the camps had been badly damaged during the bombing attack thus not providing adequate shelter. The wooden huts would cram up to 175 prisoners in a building designed to house 100.

The camps had very bad food quality consisting of rice laced with sand, rotten vegetables and meat. Not only that the rations were miniscule. All the prisoners became walking skeletons. Many contracted diseases such as beriberi and Pellagra.

Their captors provided very few hospital supplies and the hospital wards were covered in water from the leaking roofs.

Many POWs were seconded into building a new airport they were treated cruelly with a significant amount dying building the project. Those who survived were often beaten.

# I'VE GOT TO GET OUT OF HERE

## CHAPTER 10

**Sham Shi Po POW Camp**

Major John Monroe was one of many allied soldiers imprisoned at Sham Shi Po camp. It wasn't the disgusting rations, nor the inadequate leaky huts that were all crammed next to each other which drove him. What drove him was the desire to escape from this Japanese hole and become an active soldier again. He knew it was his duty as an officer to escape.

Monroe approached two fellow prisoners who he thought would be interested in joining him in his daring escape. They were Flying Officer Baugh and Captain Trevor. Captain Trevor who spoke Cantonese, they knew this would be a real asset.

Under the cover of darkness they sneaked through a hole in the barbed wire at the perimeter of the water encased camp and waded into the sea, dragging a life raft he and his fellow escapees had built from materials they found in the camp the three escapees spent an hour in the freezing water.

The three officers reached land and disappeared into the dense Chinese countryside, embarking on an epic trek across inhospitable terrain to reach China's wartime capital at Chongqing. A dangerous journey, which would take two months.

The three men knew the risk they were taking there was no doubt the Japanese would be searching for them. If caught they would be beheaded or worse still bayoneted.

They made their way across China ensuring they kept out of harms way either from the Japanese or Chinese traitors.

**Major John Monroe**

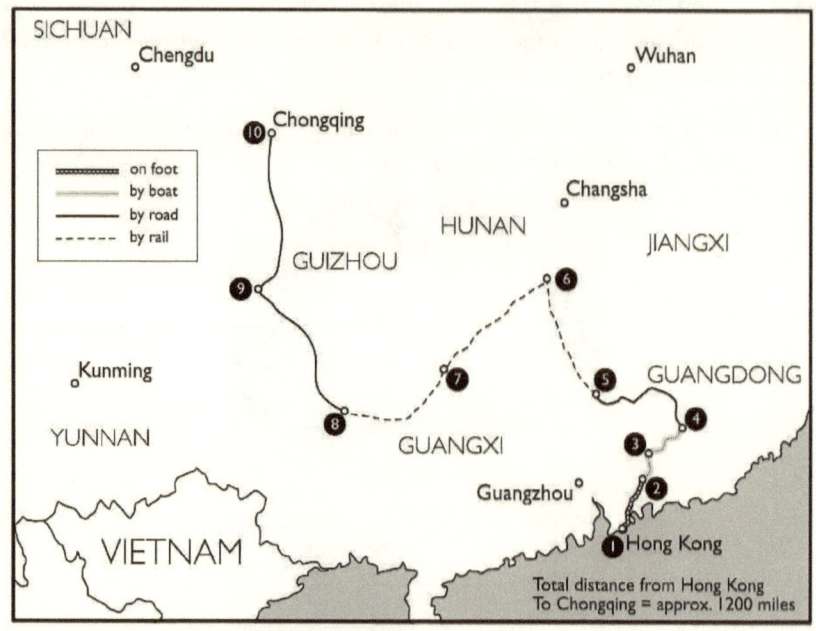

**Major John Monro's Escape Route 1942**

Town Name [present day] 1. Hong Kong 2. Waichow [Huizhou] 3. Ho Yuen [Heyuan] 4. Longchuan 5. Shaokwan [Shaoguan] 6. Hengyang 7. Kweilin [Guilin] 8. Hochee [Hechi] 9. Kweiyang [Guiyang] 10. Chungking [Chongqing]

It was difficult not to be noticed as they travelled through China they were *gweilo* round eyes.

The trek was far from easy in some places the undergrowth was thick making it difficult to descend let alone climb.

On one occasion Chinese guerrillas captured the trio. They finally convinced them they had escaped from the Japanese POW camp.

At last after a gruelling two months they reached Chongging.

**Chinese Refugees arriving in Chongging 1942**

All three re-joined the war effort.

# ESCAPE FROM JAPANESE CRUELTY

## CHAPTER 11

### December 8 1941

### Phillipines

Within ten hours of the massive attack on Pearl Harbour the Japanese embarked on an intensive aerial bombing campaign on Manila followed by a land invasion by ground troops. General Douglas MacArthur was in command of the American and Filipino troops charged with defending the archipelago, he had been recalled into active duty earlier in the year and was designated commander of the United States Armed Forces in the Asia/Pacific region.

The Japanese attack rendered his aircraft useless and the naval force assigned to protect the islands was withdrawn due to the attack on Pearl Harbour. He knew he had no chance of receiving reinforcements therefore he ordered his troops to withdraw to the Bataan Peninsula and Corregidor island at the entrance of Manila Bay.

Manila was handed over to the Japanese on January 2 1942 to prevent its complete destruction.

The U.S. and Filipino forces continued to defend until surrender was negotiated in April 1942. Over eighty thousand POWs were taken into custody.

There began one of the most disgraceful episodes in modern warfare history – the Bataan Death March.

Approximately seventy five thousand American and Filipino prisoners of war plus many Filipino citizens were assembled by their Japanese masters to embark on the Bataan Death Match. It is estimated over ten thousand didn't make it to the end dying from disease, starvation, beatings and all too often a Japanese sword or bayonet.

No matter what the prisoner's condition if they straggled behind they were murdered.

A favourite past time of the tank and truck drivers was to run over prisoners who had fallen to the ground from exhaustion.

The temperature hovered over thirty-five degrees with the humidity in the high nineties the heat together with the constant clouds of dust had the POW's craving for water. The route was dotted with artesian wells but the Japanese would not allow the prisoners to use them. If a prisoner was found drinking from a well he was either shot or beheaded. The only water the men were allowed was from the filthy carabao wallows used by the water buffalo. Dysentery was rampant. No food was given to the prisoners over the first three days of the march; finally, each man received a small ball of rice.

Dysentery was rampant. No food was given to the prisoners over the first three days of the march; finally, each man received a small ball of rice.

As the march was nearing its end about fifteen hundred men were jammed into large tin shed where the temperature rose to over forty degrees Celsius. There was one water tap, as a consequence many died while many others lost their minds.

The POWs finally reached their destination, Camp O'Donnell a former Filipino army camp north of Manila. If the prisoners thought things could only get better they were mistaken. The Japanese guards practiced the same level of barbaric cruelty as they did on the march.

In the first two months at the camp sixteen hundred Americans and sixteen thousand Filipinos died of starvation, disease or beatings by the guards. Many were executed in front of their comrades.

After a couple of months some prisoners were moved to another camp, Cabanatuan, included in the group was Sam Grashio a pilot and his Wing Commander Ed Dyess.

Cabanatuan was not an improvement over O'Donnell the rations were just as meagre and the guards were just as cruel.

Sam and Ed survived the prison but many didn't. After four

months they, and another one thousand POWs who were judged fit to work were sent to Dravo on the southern island of Mindanao.

As the march was nearing its end about fifteen hundred men were jammed into large tin shed where the temperature rose to over forty degrees Celsius. There was one water tap, as a consequence many died while many others lost their minds.

In the first two months at the camp sixteen hundred Americans and sixteen thousand Filipinos died of starvation, disease or beatings by the guards. Many were executed in front of their comrades.

After a couple of months some prisoners were moved to another camp, Cabanatuan, included in the group was Sam Grashio a pilot and his Wing Commander Ed Dyess.

Dysentery was rampant. No food was given to the prisoners over the first three days of the march; finally, each man received a small ball of rice.

As the march was nearing its end about fifteen hundred men were jammed into large tin shed where the temperature rose to over forty degrees Celsius. There was one water tap, as a consequence many died while many others lost their minds.

In the first two months at the camp sixteen hundred Americans and sixteen thousand Filipinos died of starvation, disease or beatings by the guards. Many were executed in front of their comrades.

After a couple of months some prisoners were moved to another camp, Cabanatuan, included in the group was Sam Grashio a pilot and his Wing Commander Ed Dyess.

Cabanatuan was not an improvement over O'Donnell the rations were just as meagre and the guards were just as cruel.

Sam and Ed survived the prison but many didn't. After four months they, and another one thousand POWs who were judged fit to work were sent to Dravo on the southern island of Mindanao.

The prisoners were put to work farming, logging and other forms of manual work. The work was hard but the living conditions were an improvement on the previous two prisons. Despite the easing of the punishment and better conditions only half the prisoners were in a fit state to work six months after arriving at Davao.

Originally part of the Philippine prison system, Dravo was a maximum-security prison along the lines of France's Devil's Island but instead of water, Dravo's barrier was an impenetrable malaria-infested swamp containing wild natives, poisonous snakes and crocodiles.

Dravo was situated within about one hundred and forty miles of arable land possessing fruit and nut orchards, vegetable and grain fields, and a mahogany forest worked by the prisoners. Upon conquering the Philippines, the Japanese Army took the prison to house POWs.

# Dravo Prison Philippines

The Japanese had every reason to believe escape was impossible. In the ten years of Dravos existence, no prisoner had ever escaped. In addition, roughly thirteen hundred miles of ocean separated the POWs from nearest allied country, Australia. But escape is exactly what these men had in mind. Initially there were two independent escape teams, one led by McCoy and the other by the Marines. They learned of each other's plans and joined forces. From the middle of February to the end of March 1943, and with the help of a couple of sympathetic Filipino nationals, the men secretly smuggled out the items they'd need and buried them at the agreed jump-off site. No one else in the camp knew of their plan, secrecy was essential.

On Sunday morning, April 4, with musette bags filled with last- minute items slung over their shoulders, the men assembled to take part in their work details. As a guard checked them off on a blackboard, the men marched through the gate, ostensibly on their way to their assigned field of work.

**Musette Bag**

As they did so, Frank Carpenter, an officer friend of Mellnik's shouted out jokingly, 'Hey, Steve! Your toothbrush is sticking out of the back of your musette bag. Are you planning to escape?'

Mellnik ignored the comment. Though Carpenter didn't know it, that's exactly what the men were doing.

Thirty minutes later they rendezvoused at a plougher's shack where they had secretly hidden supplies. At 10:30am they met up with two Filipinos who had agreed to guide them through the impenetrable swamp around Dravo. The men began cutting through the thick vegetation with their machetes it was very slow going.

At 6:00 p.m. the POWs assembled for the evening roll call. The guards began counting; something was wrong, they did a recount and then a third. Bafflement gave way to a stunning realization. The unthinkable had happened – ten American POWs had escaped!

The Japanese commander was furious threatening the POWs who had shared a barracks with the escapees with death. The guards beat the camp commander and the barracks leaders in a vain attempt to extract information. They all knew nothing.

Inside each Daveo barracks, 150 to 200 POWs were sardined into 15-foot intervals of space called "bays." There were approximately 16 bays per barracks, eight on each side.

The first two days in the swamp was hell for the escapees their strength was much diminished. Despite having a compass, initially they got lost and found themselves going in circles. Better progress was made when they worked out a relay system where two men would hack away at the underbrush with bolos before being relieved.

Compass readings taken at regular intervals ensured they maintained a north-easterly course.

On their second day of freedom, as evening approached, the morale of some of the exhausted men, some sick some delirious, collapsed. Dyess, as one of the original instigators of the escape, knew he should say something to improve the morale of the men, but felt Sam Grashio would be the better person as he was the most religious member of the group. Grashio, a Catholic, went to his knees and began reciting the "Memorare," a prayer to the Virgin Mary, pausing after each sentence, allowing the others to repeat it:

> *Remember, O most gracious Virgin Mary, never was it*
>
> *known that anyone who fled to your protection or sought*
>
> *your intercession was left unaided. Inspired by this*
>
> *confidence I fly unto you O Virgin of virgins, my Mother; to*
>
> *you I come, before you I stand, sinful and sorrowful. O*
>
> *Mother of the Word Incarnate, despise not my petitions, but*
>
> *in your mercy and kindness, hear and answer me. Amen."*

Grashio's words had the desired effect. None of the escapees would ever be able to explain just what had happened that night – but Grashio knew.

'I thought a miracle had occurred,' he would say. 'I felt now that God would save us.'

Four days later, they arrived at the village of Lungaog where they were greeted by Filipino guerrillas who agreed to help them get to Australia. The Filipinos guided them on a three hundred mile journey to a point where they could rendezvous with an Australian submarine and taken back to the Australian mainland and safety. The reception they received along the way was tremendous they were treated like celebrities

*Grashio recalled 'After 12 months of brutality, starvation,*

*and degradation, an abrupt change to such hospitality left us*

*midway between tears of gratitude and utter bewilderment.'*

In Australia, Dyess, McCoy, and Mellnik were presented to Commander General MacArthur who awarded them the Distinguished Service Cross.

Newspaper reports throughout America detailed the horrors of the Bataan Death March and how the Japanese ill-treated their POWs.

# DON'T LIKE COWRA MUCH

## CHAPTER 12

Japan murdered approximately five million foreign civilians and POWs during the years 1937 to 1945. Add to that the hundreds of thousands who died from beatings, starvation and disease in the camps.

Many thousands of women and girls were raped and murdered particularly in Nanking China. Thousands more were forced into sexual slavery as "comfort women" in army brothels.

Finally, we cannot forget the terrible fate of hundreds of prisoners of war who were murdered by the Japanese Army's infamous Unit 731 in the course of horrible biological experiments.

The Japanese campaign in the Pacific was brutal and savage which the Western World could not and does not comprehend.

The order by the Japanese Army to the civilian population of the island of Saipan to kill themselves and their children rather than endure the shame of being captured underlays the Japanese Psyche. Unable to reach the Japanese villagers in time to stop this atrocity, American marines could only watch as hundreds of Japanese mothers threw their children off a cliff onto the coral below and then followed them. These child murders and civilian suicides were praised and encouraged back in Japan.

In 1942 on the Kokoda Track the Japanese and Australian forces fought a bloody battle in atrocious conditions. Not only did the Japanese murder all the Australian Diggers captured they compounded this horror by killing and eating wounded Australian soldiers.

Obviously the Japanese Government did not recognize "The Geneva Convention"

The Australians strictly observed the Geneva Convention regarding POWs.

Three years after Japan began the war in the Pacific there were two thousand two hundred and twenty three Japanese prisoners of war held captive in Australia.

The POWs were well fed, given decent medical attention, and encouraged to partake in daily exercise. In winter, extra blankets and warm underwear was issued to the POWs. Under these conditions general health improved amongst the Japanese POWs. Many had been captured in New Guinea where the Japanese army had been decimated by tropical disease and weakened by starvation. Of the twenty one thousand Australian POWs captive under the care of Japan during the Second World War most were malnourished and worked to exhaustion. Eight thousand two hundred and ninety six Diggers died in captivity.

It was not the Japanese mentality to surrender; they found such an act to be humiliating and cowardly. When the Australian forces captured many Japanese soldiers in New Guinea the POWs often gave false names so that their families would presume them dead. They were shipped back to Australia where the majority were imprisoned at Cowra in New South Wales.

Cowra also imprisoned Italian POWs captured in the Middle East. The Japanese prisoners were housed in B compound. The Australian guards were well aware of the discontent of the Japanese but were not concerned about a possible break out.

**Italian POWS**

**Cowra POW Camp**

A break out from Cowra would be extremely difficult; the prisoners had no access to weapons. An escape would involve negotiating three barbed wire perimeter fences and metres of entangled barbed wire. Six guard towers, each about nine metres high, and regularly patrolled by armed guards, dominated the camp perimeter.

The camp authorities received word from a Korean prisoner that the Japanese were planning a mass breakout. This was of great concern, they knew the camp had become overcrowded and there was considerable unrest amongst the prisoners.

The army supplied Cowra with two Vickers machine guns and many more rifles and ammunition to try and avert trouble. However, the camp administration did not increase the number of guards or hut searches.

No breakout was attempted and things seemed to settle down then, in early August camp officials began to separate the B compound inmates by relocating the junior ranks to a camp at Hay in western New South Wales.

Having been informed of the prisoner transfer on 4th August, Sergeant Major Kanazawa, the commander of B compound called a meeting of the twenty hut leaders.

He asked the leaders to return to their huts and gauge the level of support for a mass breakout.

There was much debate amongst the prisoners and although it was not a majority decision, the outcome was to launch a mass escape.

The escape plan called for all injured or incapacitated prisoners to commit suicide; this would allow them to restore their honour.

It was also agreed that no civilian would be harmed.

A bugle blast at 2.00 a.m would signal the breakout and all the huts would be torched

The prisoners were armed with camp cutlery and baseball bats. They had protection against the barbed wire fences by wearing baseball mitts and using blankets.

**Broadway**

The prisoners planned to 'hit' the wire in four groups. Two groups would scale the outer three fences and negotiate the ten metres of entangled and concertina barbed wire which lay there. The other two groups would break into Broadway, so called because of its bright lights at night. One of these groups would attempt to link up with the Japanese officers in D compound, while the other would attack the outer gates and the Australian garrison, which lay beyond.

The war cries of over one thousand Japanese prisoners of war soon woke the guards; as they scrambled out of their beds they could smell the putrid smoke from the huts.

The bright lights of Broadway were soon expired by a bullet hitting the main electricity line.

The two new Vickers machine guns were put to use firing into the first wave of escapees however, the two young privates operating them were overwhelmed by the weight of numbers and were killed. Private Jones, before he was bashed to death, hid the gunlocks making the Vickers useless. His quick thinking denied the Japanese taking command of the camp.

**Funeral of Private Jones - Cowra**

The other three groups broke through the barbed wire fences. The prisoners in Broadway came under Australian fire from both ends and were pinned down for several hours. The attempt to link up with the officers in D Compound failed.

By contrast, almost all of the Japanese who crossed the perimeter wire outside B Compound escaped to freedom. Three hundred and thirty were on the loose.

It took nine days to recover them some travelled as far as Eugowra, a distance of over fifty kilometres.

**HEARING AIDS**

## Sunday Telegraph

*OVER 300,000 SOLD WEEKLY*

**Special TIME**

# WAR PRISONERS ESCAPE FROM CAMP

## Wide search by troops, police

*From Our Special Representative*

Armed soldiers and civilian police are scouring the Cowra district for prisoners of war who escaped yesterday morning.

The men broke away from the prisoner-of-war camp near Cowra at 2 a.m.

Residents in homesteads and isolated districts have been warned to keep their children and womenfolk

**ALLIED ARMIES PUSH ON**

### Allies move swiftly on French ports

LONDON, Sat — American forces thrusting south in France are expected to reach St. Nazaire and cut off the whole Brittany Penin-

The Royal Australian Air Force, police, Australian Military Force trainees and members of the Australian Women's Battalion stationed at Cowra all assisted with the roundup operations. Many escapees chose to take their own lives rather than be recaptured. Two threw themselves under an oncoming train, while many hanged themselves. On their recapture, some pleaded to be shot. Others surrendered peacefully. Local civilians and several military personnel shot at least two prisoners.

Lieutenant Harry Doncaster became the only Australian killed in the roundup, when he was attacked and murdered by a Japanese prisoner eleven kilometres north of Cowra. In total, two hundred and thirty one Japanese soldiers and officers were killed. One Japanese officer and one hundred and seven other Japanese soldiers were wounded. Four Australians had died. Four others were injured. The leaders of the breakout had ordered that no civilians be harmed, and they were true to their word.

# HOLZMINDEN

## CHAPTER 13

**Holzminden Perimeter Fence**

Every POW dreams of escape and that dream was even more intense at Holzminden; the punishment meted out by Niemeyer made the prisoners determined that they would escape this hellhole.

Niemeyer had earned a reputation as a cruel camp commandant.

A plan was devised to tunnel out beyond the perimeter fence and into a rye field. The tunnel was to begin at the foot of the staircase in the orderlies' quarters, *Kaserne B*, which was the closest block to the fence.

All officers were strictly forbidden from entering the orderlies' quarters mainly due to the fact that this was the closest point to the perimeter fence. There were guards stationed directly opposite plus the guards manning the towers had a clear view. The problem they faced was exiting the officers' quarters walking along the exterior of the building and entering the orderlies' quarters. They overcame this problem by borrowing the orderly's uniforms and waiting for a signal from their own sentries (orderlies) that the coast was clear. This method worked well and they never had a problem getting into the place where the tunnel was being dug.

After several plans were rejected as being too risky including tunnelling past the punishment cells, a new plan was devised. There was an area next to the cellar stairs that had been barricaded off with very thick boards. It had been constructed as a security measure so prisoners could not hide and "jump" the guard on duty. The fact that it was next to the stairs would indicate that the void under the stairs would be adequate to be the tunnel entrance.

The only problem was the officers did not have any proper tools to pry the boards off and replace them neatly enough to avoid detection.

They devised a plan to break a door so that the prison had to call in a village carpenter to repair it. They knew that all his tools would be counted both before and after the work was completed. One of the officers started a verbal fight with the guard and while the wild ruckus was going on another officer stole the tools they needed. The guard discovered the theft immediately but no amount of searching could discover where they had been hidden. This put the guard in a dilemma: if he reported the theft he would be accused of dereliction of duty and locked away for some time in the punishment cells. He decided to "save his own skin" and keep his mouth shut. He paid the carpenter a bribe to purchase new tools.

The officers now had all the tools needed for the job, they decided to remove the boards between 12 noon and 3pm as this was when the camp took its siesta and all apart from the guards on duty would disappear including Commandant Niemeyer.

While two officers kept watch another two started to remove the boards, this was not an easy task, as they had to complete it in total silence so as not to alert the guards.

They managed to remove all the boards and to their delight, found the space to be about four yards by five and the ceiling height was just less than six feet. This would be a perfect spot to start their tunnel to freedom.

They had to replace the boards and incorporate a door which could not be detected once this was completed they returned to their own quarters.

Every day from then on the tunnelling team went to room twenty-four, changed into their orderlies' uniforms. There were a number of scouts placed strategically around the camp to keep a lookout and give the "all clear' signal to the tunnelers.

The officers would then make their way along the building and enter the orderlies' quarters to begin their tunnelling shift.

When day's digging was complete they would use the same methodology to return to their own quarters. If there were guards in close proximity, other officers or orderlies would distract them with conversation or some pretext.

Although there were a few close calls including Niemeyer coming to the building next to the orderlies' quarters while they were digging. Overall, all went well throughout the months of tunnelling.

The code of secrecy was absolute; tunnelers would not divulge what they were doing to their fellow officers in the next bunk let alone the others sharing the hut. There may have been suspicions but nobody knew what exactly was going on.

The tunnelling process was taking a long time; their hours of work were very much restricted by the camp regime of roll call and the issue of the daily potato ration from the adjoining cellar. Work therefore could not begin until after 11am and end well before the 4pm roll call.

The tunnelers worked in almost complete darkness and the smell, which greeted them each day, was putrid; stale air, dampness and sweat.

The worst part was putting on their damp wet mud encrusted digging clothes, which was worn in the tunnel.

They encountered a number of obstacles that could have proved to be fatal to the tunnel's completion but ingenuity and hard work overcame them.

The final obstacle was the building's foundation, which were constructed with concrete and sitting on solid rock. In a normal situation one would use a jackhammer and bolt cutters to break through the steel reinforcing. The tunnelers only had kitchen knives, spoons, penknives and anything else they could find to tunnel. There was a cold chisel from the stolen carpenter's tools, which did help, but it was not going to complete the task.

One thing they had learned from living in Germany was fifty marks could buy you most things. They bribed a village workman who was working in the camp to supply some sulphuric acid. Fashioning some clay cups enabled them to pour the acid on the steel reinforcing rods, which melted the rods allowing them through.

Once through the foundations they turned north heading for the perimeter fence and out past the prison grounds to the rye field. It was essential they came up in the field and not open ground as the guards would spot them with the aid of their searchlights; the escapees would be sitting ducks.

The tunnel was not much more than a rabbit hole, it was sixteen inches wide and twelve inches high; the tunnelers had to wriggle through, certainly not crawl. There was no other way to dig, as the amount of earth extracted had to be limited as it all had to be hidden in the cellar. Each digger was allocated one candle as they were very hard to obtain, each man had to move along in pitch black until they reached their allotted location and then light the candle and begin digging.

As in any man made tunnel it had to be reinforced with timber planks all of which were stolen. These came not only from the tunnelers beds but other POWs in the hut also. Many a complaint was made including by the tunnelling team but the mystery of the missing boards was never solved.

Once the boards had been seconded and were in the tunnel, they had to be secured which was an exhausting process. They had to be cut to the right size as the measurements differed along the tunnel. A tunneler would drag a board along the tunnel to the point where it was required. He would have to roll on his back holding the board in place with one hand and with the other hand wedge an upright board under one end to brace it. Nothing was easy about tunnelling out of Holzminden.

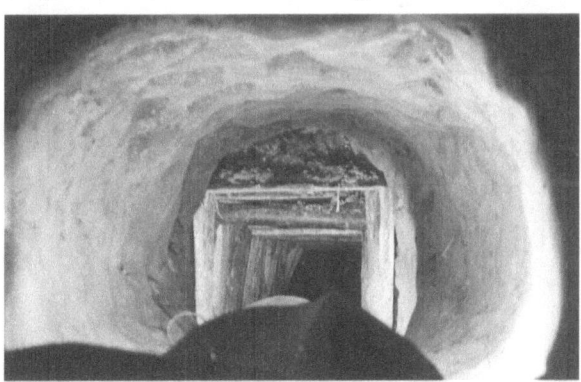

**Holzminden Escape Tunnel**

When a tunneler had filled his soil bowl he would lift himself up as far as the twelve-inch ceiling of the tunnel would allow and pass it under his body. He would then tug on the rope to signal to the man at the end of the tunnel to haul it out. The soil would be shovelled into pillowcases stolen from the living quarters and stacked against the cellar walls. When the cellar was full they hauled the bags up to the attic or filled their pockets and stored it under the roof tiles.

At the end of the day at 3.45pm, the three man digging team had to be out of the tunnel. They changed back into their orderlies' uniforms and returned in the same manner as they arrived in the morning with scouts looking out for guards and their mates manning the doors. Once inside their quarters they changed into their normal uniforms.

The 4pm roll call came and went without incident.

As they were nearing the completion of the tunnel Commandant Niemeyer had grown suspicious of an escape and increased the number of guards outside the perimeter fence with one stationed directly over the spot where the tunnel would emerge.

Colonel Rathborne, the senior officer, decided to dig another tunnel off the main tunnel heading north instead of west, which was the original route. This would require them to dig a much longer tunnel to reach the rye crops they needed for cover.

They were required to dig another fifty meters to reach the rye but progress was slow as rocks and roof collapses were slowing their pace down to two feet a day. The supply of timber boards was also slowing up so they were forced to take risks.

They were racing against time as the rye crop was due to be harvested in early August and they couldn't afford to lose their cover.

# BREAK OUT

## CHAPTER 14

At last the tunnel was complete, it was decided that one of the officers, Lieutenant Butler, would make his way to the end of the tunnel dig up until he broke the earth and wave a little white flag for two seconds. The officers in the barracks would keep watch and identify where exactly the tunnel exit would be.

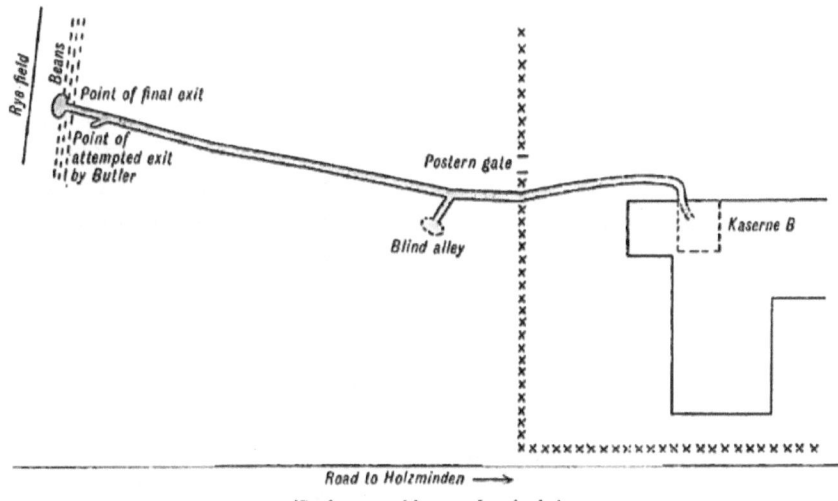

(Scale = roughly 40 yds = inch.)

The officers watched in horror as the flag was waved in a bean field ten yards short of the rye. There was little chance they could dig the extra distance before the rye was harvested so they decided to work with what they had. The beans did give some protection although not as much as their original target.

The night of the escape arrived at last; there was excitement and tension in *Kaserne A* as the men of the tunnelling team prepared to enter the tunnel. None of the men were told their allocated sequence so as not to create too much tension and excitement. They were instructed to go to bed fully clothed and be ready to go when they were tapped on the shoulder.

The final barracks inspection was at 10pm both barrack doors were then locked.

The escapees had to climb through a hole cut in the attic of the officers' quarters and crawl along the ceiling eaves until they reached the trapdoor in the orderlies' section. An Australian Lieutenant, Louis Grieve, was working as the "doorman' at the hole in the attic. He would not permit the next man to pass through until he received word that the last man had passed through the tunnel entrance.

Grieve was a big burly man so no one was going to argue with him.

The first man to exit the tunnel was Lieutenant Butler, he was allocated the task of "breaking out" he used a bread knife that had been stolen from the kitchen to dig out a six inch hole large enough for him to stick his head out and observe the lay of the land. He was delighted to discover the exit was in the middle of the bean field and not far from the rye.

The arc lights illuminated the perimeter fence and beyond. He heard a cough and quickly looked in that direction it was a guard. Butler was out of the light so he hoped he had been spotted. He waited for a minute but the guard had not moved. He spent the next thirty minutes widening the exit hole and then pushed his escape kit out and made for the rye field. He noticed that not far away was a guard snoring; obviously sound asleep. He was oblivious to the fact there was a major escape happening right under his nose.

The other two men in Butler's group were Langren and Clouston, they exited the tunnel soon after Butler. It was 11.45pm and the heavy rain that had been falling throughout the night had ceased. There was a full moon and it now started to shine through the clouds. The increased light together with the fact that the rye was now ripe making a loud crackling noise when touched did not improve their chances of getting away undetected.

It was decided to make their way through the beans until they reached a point where they needed to cross a large field. Just then, it started to rain again quite heavily and the noise of the rain on the rye allowed them to proceed without being heard. At the far side of the field they stopped to put on their rucksacks and looked back at Holzminden; they all hoped for the last time.

Reaching the river they discovered a raft; loading it up with their rucksacks and their clothing they pushed it across the river. The three men then made off in a north-westerly direction heading for the Dutch frontier.

While Butler and his comrades were making good their escape, the rest of the escapees were working their way through the tunnel and crawling into the beans and other crops. Most of them were in groups of three.

The escapees went off in different directions, some even moving east towards Berlin to confuse the Germans. The officers who spoke fluent German chose to travel by train speeding up their exit from the enemy territory.

The original thirteen man tunnelling team were now through the tunnel, it was now the turn of Colonel Rathborne and six supplementary officers. He was a portly man and found it extremely difficult to get through the tunnel with his kit being pushed in front; he made it. The other six entered the tunnel every few minutes with the last man out being James Bennett. All up, twenty-nine had been able to traverse the tunnel and make their escape.

**Lieutenant Cecil Blain, Captain David Gray**

**and Lieutenant Caspar Kennard**

All three made it to freedom wearing these outfits.

**Escape Tunnel Discovered**

The thirtieth man was not so fortunate, the tunnel collapsed in on him and the man behind had to drag him out. The tunnel was inspected and the decision was reluctantly taken that there would be no more escapes that night. The remaining prisoners, fifty in all, had to return to their beds bitterly disappointed and not looking forward to the morning when roll call was taken; they knew retribution that would be taken. The tunnel was closed and the secret hatches and doors sealed so the guards would not find them in their search. In the mad rush to exit the tunnel by 6am they had to leave two escapees until the roll call had been completed. Once freed, they raced back to their barracks not by the safe route but straight out the door of the orderlies' quarters. They ran into Niemeyer conducting an impromptu inspection, he questioned them both but did not ask them why their uniforms were so soiled. Just then, Niemeyer heard local farmers yelling to him from the other side of the perimeter fence. He approached them to hear their grievances, they were angry about their crops being crushed and trampled. This sent alarm bells ringing in Niemeyer's head he demanded the gates be opened and he and several guards went to inspect the damage. It was easy to discover the exit hole and Niemeyer ordered a guard to enter the tunnel and trace it back to its source. The guard refused not willing to take the risk of discovering escapees still in the tunnel. He placed a guard at the exit hole and returned to camp to report the escape to his superiors in Hanover. He dispatched one of his men to complete a headcount the guard returned and reported twenty-nine missing. Niemeyer's jaw dropped, he turned grey it seemed he had aged ten years in that very instant. He then began to yell and rant in a ridiculous manner, you could hear the laughter emanating from the prisoners barracks.

Niemeyer immediately ordered all doors to be locked and issued "safety of camp" orders, all prisoners were confined to barracks and their rooms with all communication between prisoners banned. He also issued orders to his guards that if they saw anybody at the windows, to shoot them! This actually happened when he spotted an officer looking out. He ordered a guard to shoot narrowly missing he officer and shattering the window. There were more shots fired at the building and one prisoner received a flesh wound from a bayonet; all in all total chaos! One of the officers rigged up a dummy attached to a rope, which could be moved up and down in front of the window. There was much firing of rifles and shattering of glass and laughter inside the barracks.

For the next month life inside the camp was "hell on earth" for the prisoners, the punishment cells were full of officers incarcerated for doing nothing and beatings became a regular occurrence. The local villagers hearing about the escape would gather outside the fence as though they were an audience at a circus. This infuriated Niemeyer even more, he believed they were mocking him.

He instituted new procedures where guards would inspect inside the barracks three times a night shining a bright torch into each prisoner's eyes. Sleep deprivation became a real issue.

If these conditions were not bad enough "Spanish Flu" was sweeping throughout Germany and the rest of the world. Several officers died from the pandemic although other camps suffered up to one thousand deaths.

In the meantime, the escapees were all making their way to the Dutch border some hiding for twenty-one hours and only travelling in the dead of night for the remaining three. With the aid of home-made compasses and a map smuggled into the camp from England they managed to find their way. An Australian officer who had been a photographer before the war duplicated the map. He managed to bribe locals with food from Red Cross parcels for photographic equipment. Each team had a copy of this very detailed map.

Of the twenty-nine who escaped, ten made it to Holland and their freedom, the nineteen who were recaptured were all tried and convicted; they were sentenced to six months imprisonment in a civilian gaol. Because the Armistice was close their sentences was never enforced.

Even after the "great escape" prisoners were attempting to break out of the camp; another tunnel had been dug.

# COLDITZ

## CHAPTER 15

**Colditz Castle**

**Photo Taken 1945**

Colditz Castle is a Renaissance castle in the town of Colditz near Leipzig, Dresden and Chemnitz in the state of Saxony in Germany. The castle was used as a workhouse for the poor. It was also home for the mentally sick for over 100 years. It became the most famous Prisoner of War prison during the Second World War housing the "incorrigible" Allied officers who had repeatedly escaped from other camps.

The castle lies between the towns of Hartha and Grimma on a spur over the Zwickauer Mulde and had the first wildlife park in Germany.

In 1046, Henry III of the Holy Roman Empire gave the burghers of Colditz permission to build the first documented settlement at the site. In 1083, Henry IV urged Margrave Wiprecht of Groitzsch to develop the castle site, which Colditz accepted. In 1158, Emperor Frederick Barbarossa made Thimo I "Lord of Colditz", and major building works began. By 1200, the town around the market was established. Forests, empty meadows, and farmland were settled next to the pre-existing Slavic villages Zschetzsch, Zschadraß, Zollwitz, Terpitzsch and Koltzschen.

Around that time the larger villages Hohnbach, Thierbaum, Ebersbach and Tautenhain also emerged.

In the Middle Ages, the castle played an important role as a lookout post for the German Emperors and was the centre of the Reich territories of the Pleißenland (anti-Meißen Pleiße-lands). In 1404, the nearly 250-year rule of the dynasty of the Lords of Colditz ended when Thimo VIII sold Colditz Castle for 15,000 silver marks to the Wettin ruler of the period in Saxony.

Various renovations were completed through the Middle Ages, it was also rebuilt in 1504 when a fire which began in the bakery razed the castle to the ground.

In the 19th century, the church space was rebuilt in the neo-classic architectural style, but its condition was allowed to deteriorate. The castle was used by Frederick Augustus III, Elector of Saxony as a workhouse to feed the poor, the ill, and persons under arrest. It served this purpose from 1803 to 1829, when its workhouse function was taken over by an institution in Zwickau. In 1829, the castle became a mental hospital for the "incurably insane" from Waldheim. In 1864, a new hospital building was erected in the Gothic Revival style, on the ground where the stables and working quarters had been previously located. It remained a mental institution until 1924.

The castle was home to several notable figures during its time as a mental institution, including Ludwig Schumann, the second youngest son of the famous composer Robert Schumann and Ernst Baumgarten, one of the original inventors of the airship.

When the Nazis came to power in 1933, they turned the castle into a political prison for communists, homosexuals, Jews and other "undesirables". Beginning in 1939 allied prisoners was housed there.

After the outbreak of World War II the castle was converted into a high security prisoner-of-war camp for officers who had become security or escape risks or who were regarded as particularly dangerous. Since the castle is situated on a rocky outcrop above the River Mulde, the Germans believed it to be an ideal site for a high security prison.

The larger outer courtyard, known as the Kommandantur, had only two exits and housed a large German garrison. The prisoners lived in an adjacent courtyard in a ninety-foot (twenty seven meter) tall building. Outside, the flat terraces which surrounded the prisoners' accommodation were constantly watched by armed sentries and surrounded by barbed wire. Although known as Colditz Castle to the locals, its official German designation was Oflag IV-C and it was under Wehrmacht control.

Although it was considered a high security prison, it boasted one of the highest records of successful escape attempts. This could be owing to the general nature of the prisoners that were sent there; most of them had attempted escape previously from other prisons and were transferred to Colditz because the Germans had thought the castle escape-proof.

In April 1945, US troops entered Colditz town and, after a two-day fight, captured the castle on 16 April. In May 1945, the Soviet occupation of Colditz began. Following the Yalta Conference it became a part of East Germany. The Soviets turned Colditz Castle into a prison camp for local burglars and non-communists. Later, the castle was a home for the aged and nursing home, as well as a hospital and psychiatric clinic. For many years after the war, forgotten hiding places and tunnels were found by repairmen, including a radio room set up by the British POWs, which was then "lost" again only to be re-discovered some ten years later.

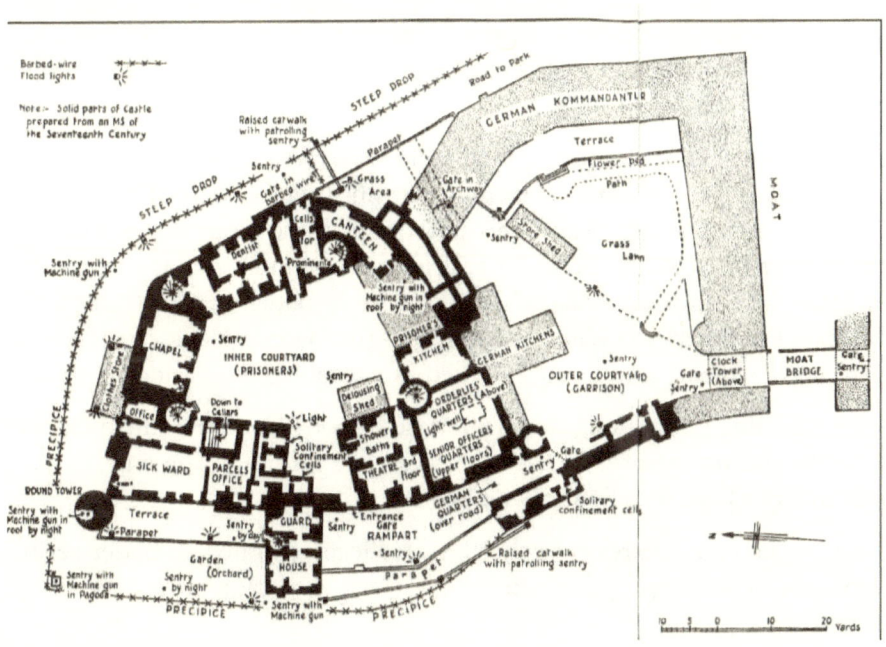

# Reach for the Sky

## Douglas Bader - Guest of Colditz

Douglas Bader was born in London, England on February 21, 1910. His father, Frederick Bader, was a civil engineer and his mother Jessie, played Mah-jong.

The first two years of young Doug's life was spent with relatives on the Isle of Man as his parents were living in India due to Fred's work commitments. Douglas joined his parents in India from the age of two until returning home to Britain a year later. The family settled in London. In 1914 with the outbreak of World War I, Bader's father joined the military. Frederick was badly wounded in the Battle of Passchendaele in 1917 he was repatriated home but died as a result of his wounds in 1922.

Jessie did not grieve long and re-married soon after. She and her new husband did not want a little twelve year old getting in the way, he was sent to Saint Edward's School as a border.

His class had an excursion to the RAF College at Cranwell; Bader set his sights on becoming a pilot and won a place as a cadet at RAF College Cranwell.

Bader was commissioned as an Officer in the Royal Air Force in 1930 and was posted to 23 Squadron at RAF Kenley. Bader demonstrated great ability as a pilot in fact he was selected to fly in the Squadron's aerobatic display team at the prestigious RAF Hendon display in 1931.

His reputation for taking risks was well known particularly in low level aerobatics. In December 1931, Bader crashed during an unauthorized low-level aerobatic routine at Woodley while visiting the Reading Aero Club. He survived the crash although he came close to death. He had both his legs amputated.

Doctors fitted him with artificial "tin" legs soon, Bader learned to walk without the use of a stick and was not only driving his car but also flying.

Douglas was certified by the Central Flying School as perfectly able to fly however, the Air Force had no precedent to guide them, they could only offer him a ground based commission.

Bader resigned and found work with the Asiatic Petroleum Company.

Douglas didn't enjoy civilian life although he was happily married and was the only golfer with tin legs playing from a ten handicap at his club.

With the outbreak of the Second World War Bader applied to rejoin the RAF. With pilots in short supply they accepted his application by June 1940 Bader had been posted to command 242 Squadron, which had suffered badly in The Battle of France.

**Bader and Wingman From the 242**

He knew he had to raise morale; Bader's methods were typically uncompromising. His management skills brought the 242 back into an effective fighting unit.

Bader made an impact on The Battle of Britain with his aggressive tactics and the determination of his squadron. He was promoted to Wing Commander in 1941 and was stationed at RAF Tangmere, he lead the

"Tangmere Wing" in sweeps over North West Europe aimed to bring the Luftwaffe into combat. By the summer of 1941 Bader had claimed twenty two victories making him the fifth highest scoring pilot in the RAF.

Bader was flying over France in August 1941 when German fighters shot him down. Bader bailed out from his damaged machine and parachuted to the ground but both his artificial legs were badly damaged.

Bader was captured by German forces and was taken to a hospital near St Omer where his damaged artificial legs were repaired. The German hospital staff feeling sympathy for the legless pilot allowed Bader to retain his clothing. French villagers helped him break out from hospital! The locals escorted him to a farm but someone betrayed him and he was re-arrested. Taking no further chances, the Germans put Bader under close guard and he was sent to a Prisoner of War camp. Eventually he arrived at Colditz as a result of his constant and unremitting hostility to his captors. Bader remained in captivity despite numerous escape attempts until Colditz was liberated in 1945.

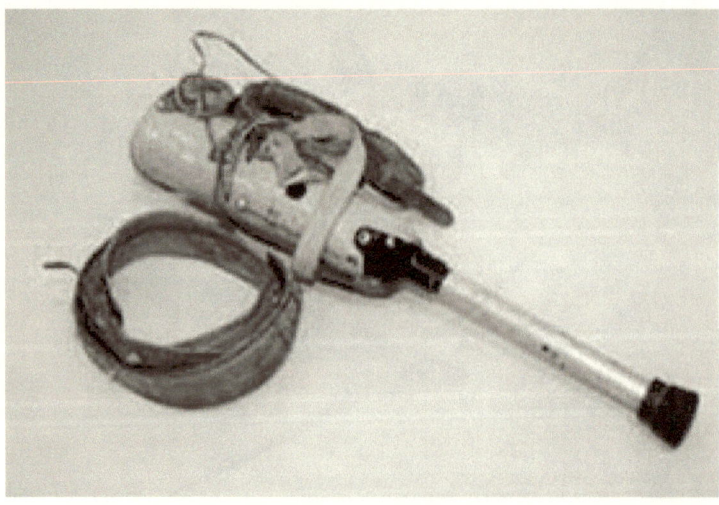

**Bader's Tin Leg**

# LOVE CONQUERS THE WALL

## CHAPTER 16

**Horace Greasly**

Horace Greasley was born on Christmas Day in 1918 along with twin brother Harold, to Joseph and Mabel Greasley. The Greasley twins grew up in the village of Ibstock, where they worked on their family's farm.

Horace and Harold were inseparable and both boys were popular with the girls of the village not only for their good looks but their bravado bordering on larrikinism.

Both enjoyed working on the family farm where they kept dairy cattle and pigs. In both their minds living on a farm for the rest of their lives would suit them down to the ground.

Circumstances changed, the farm could not sustain them both so Horace left the farm to become a hairdresser. He was cutting the mayors hair when news came in that Hitler's army had invaded Czechoslovakia. He knew immediately that he would be liable to be called up along with Harold.

They were both conscripted in the first draft.

Soon after his call up notification was received a regular client offered to get him a job as a fireman, a reserved occupation which would actually pay better than joining the services and would keep him out of the firing line. Horace turned the offer down.

Both twins trained with the 2nd/5th Battalion Leicestershire Regiment and were dispatched off to France as part of the British Expeditionary Force.

Horace and Harold had no idea what they were in for.

The German and Allied forces were roughly evenly matched. The Germans offensive fielded one hundred and thirty six divisions against ninety-four French divisions, and ten British divisions of the British Expeditionary Force. Twenty-two Belgian and nine Dutch divisions completed the allied forces. The numbers of tanks fielded on each side was also approximately equal. It was only in the air that the Germans enjoyed massive superiority: two thousand five hundred aircraft against a few hundred British, and largely obsolete French aircraft.

The quantity of the Allied troops was fine; the quality was not. Britain and France had been largely unprepared for war, and the training of their conscript armies was abysmal. In Britain, ammunition shortages meant each recruit was allowed only five rounds in total for rifle training. The French conscripts were even less trained. Fortunately, the small British Expeditionary Force had many professional troops to reinforce the recent conscripts.

By contrast the Germans had had much more intensive and elaborate training. Hitler knew there would be a war! Accurate, full-scale mock-ups of crucial fortifications were built in Germany, and troops rehearsed their attacks until perfect.

The Allies were defeated, the High Command knew they had to evacuate over three hundred and fifty thousand men including the British French and Belgian divisions who were trapped in the port of Dunkirk. The British decided to evacuate them by sea. Initially, they believed that they would be able to rescue, about thirty thousand men. Over the course of ten incredible days from May 26 to June 4, they accomplished a magnificent feat. The navy put out a call for help from the civilian population and boats from all over Britain began appearing

Fishing boats, yachts, pleasure boats, rowboats, all answered the call. Under constant aerial attack the navy and civilians evacuated nearly Three hundred and forty thousand men. They had to leave behind all of their heavy equipment but that could be replaced. When it was over, Britain still had an army with which to fight another day.

For every seven soldiers who escaped through Dunkirk, one man was left behind as a prisoner of war (POW). The majority of these prisoners were sent on forced marches into Germany. Horace was one of those captured.

What followed was a ten week forced march across France and Belgium to Holland and a three-day train journey to prison camps in Polish Silesia, then annexed as part of Germany. Many died on the way, Greasley reckoned himself lucky to have survived.

In the second POW camp to which he was assigned, near Lamsdorf, he encountered the seventeen year-old daughter of the director of the marble quarry to which the camp was attached.

She was working, as an interpreter for the Germans There was a mutual attraction between Horace and this beautiful young girl.

Within a few weeks Horace and Rosa were having an intimate relationship right under the German's noses. They would meet in all sorts of hiding places including the camp work sheds; nothing would dampen their lust for each other. Unfortunately after one year of their relationship Horace was transferred to Freiwaldau, an annex of Auschwitz, some forty miles away.

**Rosa**

There was only one way to continue their lustful relationship, break out of his new camp. Security at Freiwaldau was not very tight as it was located on the border of Germany and Polish Silesia; there was little hope of escaping back to Britain. The nearest neutral country was Sweden, four hundred and twenty miles to the north.

Greasley reasoned that short absences could be disguised or go unnoticed. Messages were exchanged between him and Rosa via members of village work parties and handed to Horace, the camp barber, when they had their hair cut.

Horace, with the help of mates, would go under the wire to meet Rosa, they made wild passionate love and he would break back into the camp under the cover of darkness.

Greasley recalled that in some weeks he made the return journey three or more times depending on whether Rosa's translation duties brought her close to his camp. His proven bravado to continue their love affair was not the only testimony to his daring. This photograph shows Heinrich Himmler, head of the SS, inspecting a prison camp and a shirtless skinny POW close to the fence confronting him.

**Horace Confronts Himmler**

The prisoner was Horace Greasley; he is shown with his shirt off demonstrating to Himmler that they were not being fed enough and that all the POW's were as thin as he was.

Horace had no idea who Himmler was but survived the introduction. The food rations were not increased.

Rosa did help with his nutrition by giving him food parcels to take back to the camp, she also smuggled radio parts, which enabled the prisoners to keep up with the news by listening to the BBC.

Horace broke out of camp two hundred times. He broke back in two hundred times. This made Horace Grimsley the greatest escapologist in history!

Horace was held in captivity for five years, he was finally liberated on 24 May 1945, he returned to Britain and continued the relationship with Rosa via letters soon after the war, he even provided her with a reference allowing her to work as a translator for the Americans.

Sometime after Horace returned home he received the very sad news that Rosa had died during childbirth, the newborn died as well. Although Rosa never told him of her pregnancy, he knew in his heart of hearts that the child was his. Horace was heartbroken.

The love affair conducted with Rosa was a dangerous one not only because of the constant danger of the escapes but unknown to Horace she was Jewish. If the authorities had discovered her ancestry both would have been hanged.

Horace and Rosa proved the adage "Love Conquers All"

# THE AUSSIE LARRIKIN
## WHY HITLER ORDERED WILLY SHOT

### CHAPTER 17

**Willy Williams**

Squadron Leader John "Willy" Williams was a boy from Manly, Sydney, Australia. Willy became a World War II ace and briefly, one of the youngest squadron leaders in the history of the RAF. The average life expectancy of an RAF pilot was rather short so senior pilots tended to be young.

**Willy in the Middle East**

Willy survived being shot down over France and ended up as a POW in Stalag Luft III on the German-Polish border. This was a camp purpose built to be escape proof. The commandant, Luftwaffe Colonel von Luger, told the senior British officer, Group Captain Ramsey.

'There will be no escapes from this camp.'

'It is our duty to try to escape.' replied Ramsey.

Willy would become an integral player in what became known as "The Great Escape".

The men demonstrated ingenuity along with great organization skills and mental toughness to achieve the ultimate escape. Seventy-six prisoners tunnelled out of the so-called "escape proof" camp right under the German's noses.

Willy played a major role in planning and excavating the tunnels. He did make it through the tunnel along with his good schoolmate Reginald "Rusty" Keirath.

They were both heading for Switzerland along the German Czech border when they were captured.

Hitler was so infuriated that so many had escaped he ordered the summary execution of fifty officers. Willy and Rusty died together in a dark forest at the hand of a Gestapo officer and a Luger pistol.

At the Nuremberg trials after the war twenty Gestapo officers were sentenced to hang for this atrocity.

## The Great Escape

If you were unfortunate enough to be captured by the Germans in World Two you could do a lot worse than been sent to Stalag Luft 111 (Sagan). The housing and recreational facilities were better than most prisoner of war camps.

**A Barracks at Stalag Luft 111**

British and American airmen were the predominant inmates they had mostly been shot down over Axis territory.

However, it was the sworn duty of all captured military personnel to continue to fight the enemy by surviving, communicating information and escaping. Many of the prisoners at Sagan were re-captured escapees. The Germans believed that security at the new camp would make it impossible to escape.

Many of the POWs were officers with strong organisational skills; they knew if any escape was to be successful it had to be well planned.

The prisoners at Sagan therefore established an "escape committee". The chief escape officer was Squadron Leader Roger Bushell, a former escapee who had been recaptured several times. He was known as 'Big X'.

It was decided to build three tunnels and free two hundred POWs. The tunnels were given the names of "Tom" "Dick" and "Harry".

The problem they needed to resolve was twofold, how to dispose of the dirt from the dig and how to support the tunnel to prevent it from collapsing.

Bed boards were used just as they were at Colditz; the same problem of no support for their mattresses also occurred in both camps; some rigged up hammocks.

A major problem was how to dispose of the soil from the tunnel; the colour of the soil was different from what surrounded their barracks and the camp overall.

One method they used was to manufacture long bags which could be filled with earth then hidden in the prisoner's trouser legs. A cord around the neck would open the bags thus releasing the earth on a patch of ground that was being dug or cultivated by another prisoner. Those dispersing the dirt in this way were known as "Penguins". More than one hundred tons of earth was disposed of in this way. Another method involved filling empty Red Cross boxes, placing the boxes in the middle of a group of men who would then gradually bury the earth.

An integral group within the escape group were the forgers; they were responsible for creating maps and identity papers.

Tailors were also critical to the escapee's success, they made civilian clothes out of blankets and other materials that were scrounged and altered uniforms.

The German guards discovered "Tom". This was a major blow to the success of the escape. The escape committee decided to suspend all digging in "Dick" and "Harry" until they felt safe to recommence activities.

When things settled down they were able to complete "Harry" the great escape was planned for 24th March 1944. It was a perfect moonless night to depart Sagan and the Germans hospitality!

The committee decided the only fair way to decide who went and who stayed was to draw lots.

On the fateful night the escapees congregated in hut 104, the plan was to leave the camp in stages.

One prisoner was appointed to breakout of the tunnel to ensure the exit came in the woods out of sight of the guards. He returned with disturbing news; the tunnel was about ten feet short of the woods. This would mean they were directly in the path of the guard patrolling the perimeter fence. The committees hastily met and devised a methodology, which would indicate to the man coming up through the tunnel exit that he could proceed.

Time was their enemy and it was now past 10pm, a decision was made that the escape would cease at 5am. It was also very clear with the time available that the two hundred-man target would not be met.

At 4.45am they heard rifle shots, the tunnel exit had been discovered.

Seventy-Six men had escaped through the tunnel. Those that were found waiting their turn in hut 104 were sent to the solitary confinement cells.

Of the seventy-six men who escaped, three made it home to the UK. Twenty-Three were recaptured and sent back to Sagan. Hitler personally ordered the execution of the other fifty men including Willy and Rusty.

The commandant of Stalag Luft III, Lindeiner, was court-martialled by the Gestapo for not preventing the escape.

# Billie Stephens Made a Home Run from Colditz

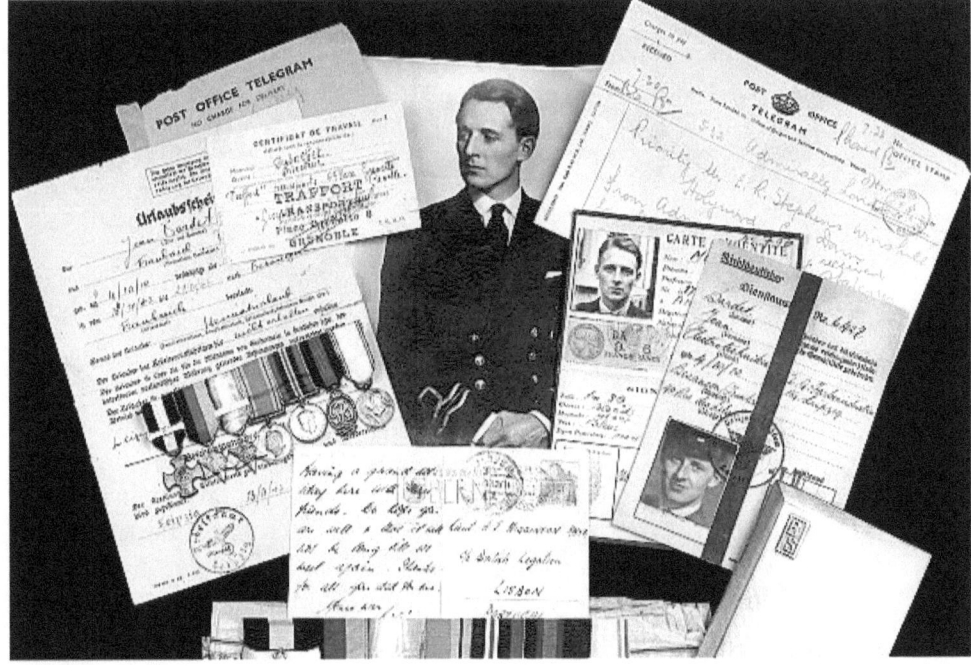

**Lieutenant Commander William "Billie" Stephens forged documents**

William (Billie) Stephens was the son of a Belfast shipping agent and timber importer. He was born in Belfast and educated at Shrewsbury before joining his father's firm. He joined the Royal Naval Volunteer Reserve in 1930 and at the outbreak of the Second World War joined the coastal forces

He received a commission to command a Motor Launch; this was a relatively small vessel measuring one hundred and twelve feet, weighing eighty-five tons and was capable of speeds up to twenty knots.

**Motor Launch 192**

Billie was heavily involved in what is now known as a famous raid on St Nazaire on the Burgundy coast on 27 March 1942. He commanded his Motor Launch 192 with considerable skill and bravery. Intelligence reports intimated that the new German battleship "Tirpitz" was now completed although in need of some last minute repairs. The size of the battleship meant the only dry dock available to her was at St Nazair on the mouth of the river Loire.

A plan was hatched, "Operation Chariot": a daring scheme whereby the destroyer Cambeltown packed with five tons of explosives would ram the gates of the dock blowing them up. Two destroyers escorted Cambletown on her mission and an armada of smaller vessels including sixteen motor launches. As Cambletown steamed full throttle towards the gates she came under extreme enemy fire however, unstoppable, she hit the lock gates at 1.30am.

The fast and manoeuvrable motor launches drew their fare share of fire, as was their mission. Only four of the sixteen returned to Britain.

Billie Stephens was in command of one of the leading motor launches they were almost abeam of the harbour wall when the launch was hit by intensive gunfire. Completely immobilised and on fire he had no option but to order his men to abandon ship. Managing to swim ashore carrying the wounded sailors they were taken prisoner by the Germans.

The Cambeltown eventually blew up destroying the main gate and killing a number of German officers.

Stephens and his crew were taken to a courtyard where they were searched and then lined up against a wall. The men knew their destiny.

Fortunately, an officer arrived and took control ensuring the safety of the prisoners. The British officers and sailors were imprisoned in an underground store without food or water despite having several wounded men. The prisoners were then transported to Stalag 133 where they endured appalling conditions. Stephens was sent to Wilhelmshaven and interrogated at great length before being sent to Marlag from where he made his first escape. En route to Oflag IV C (Colditz) Billie jumped from the train, he was captured the next day and sent on to Colditz to serve a week in solitary confinement.

Major Pat Reid, in The Colditz Story (1952) recalled his early impression of Stephens:

> 'He was handsome, fair-haired, with piercing blue eyes and Nelsonian nose. He walked as if he was permanently on the deck of a ship. He was a daredevil, and his main aim appeared to be to force his way into the German area of the camp and then hack his way out with a metaphorical cutlass.'

Five weeks later, Stephens and Major Ronnie Littledale submitted their plan to the escape committee. It was accepted. They requested two other POWs to join them one was to have lock-picking skills. Hank Wardle was chosen for this task, along with Major Reid as the second member.

They began their extensive preparation over the following days using the experiences of other successful escapes.

Reid insisted that each man carry a small suitcase to give them all a look of respectability, he thought travelling without one would signal they were fugitives.

Wearing balaclavas and socks over their shoes with their suitcases under their arms filled with sheets they began their escape.

On 14th October wearing balaclavas, gloves and socks over their shoes and carrying their suitcases muffled with blankets containing sheets, they began their escape Pat Reid led the way through a kitchen window. Once in position Reid was able to signal back to the others when the coast was clear they could then proceed through the window. The next stage was barred window, which gave them access to a flat roof well illuminated: a guard was only fifteen yards away.

The Battle of Britain pilot, Douglas Bader, was acting as an observer conducting the "Colditz Orchestra". The plan involved the orchestra pausing when a guard had his back to them. This enabled each of the four men to make a dash for the shadows of a ventilator safely. The critical next hurdle of the escape was a narrow flue. Stripping naked they managed to squeeze through. Somewhat battered and bruised they dressed in a nearby shrubbery. Strolling nonchalantly past the sleeping sentry in the barracks they continued on. Knotting the sheets they dropped in three stages, fifty-four feet in total into a dry moat.

Billie started to cough when he reached the ground bring attention to himself and the others. He quickly stuffed his mouth full of grass and dirt in an act of desperation.

The men then climbed the outer wall, which was only ten feet high. At 4am they shook hands split into two pairs and Stephens and Littledale set off together.

They strolled to a station at Rochlitz trying not to bring attention to themselves. Catching the train to Chemnitz en route to Nuremberg they changed at Hoff, where they sat in the station drinking beer. The escapees had been warned to keep away from Stuttgart; it was far too dangerous. Travelling on minor rail lines they eventually reached Tubingen. After two days of trekking they reached the Swiss border crossing under the cover of darkness. Their journey from Colditz had taken only five days. Reid and Wardle had travelled a different route arriving the day before. All were interned in Switzerland.

The Swiss released the group after questioning, Stephens made his way to France continuing on over the Pyrenees and into Spain The Spanish authorities arrested him and once again Billie found himself in prison. Billie was a charmer, he bribed a guard with his wristwatch to allow him to telephone the British Embassy in Madrid. The British smuggled him out in the boot of a Cadillac to Gibraltar and from there he flew to the UK.

After the war Stephens returned to Northern Ireland to continue with the family business. He became chairman of Northern Bank and the Northern Ireland Tourist Board as well as Commissioner of Belfast Harbour and High Sheriff of County Down. He was also involved in the Missions to Seamen.

This debonair man, full of charisma, was always immaculate, fit and alert. He had a certain magic and an excitement to him. He was absolutely devoted to his Swiss wife Chou-chou who sheltered him after he crossed the Swiss border. They delighted in entertaining their many friends and in playing endless hours of bridge and the French edition of Scrabble. In the late Eighties they moved to France, to a cottage near Nice for the sake of her health. Her death in 1993 was a severe blow to him.

Prisoners made many attempts to escape Oflag IV-C (Colditz). Approximately thirty-six men succeeded in their attempts.

The German Army made Colditz a Sonderlager (high-security prison camp), the only one of its type located within Germany. Field Marshal Hermann Göring declared Colditz "escape-proof" yet despite this audacious claim, there were multiple escapes by British, Australian, Canadian, French, Polish, Dutch, and Belgian inmates. Despite some misapprehensions to the contrary, Colditz Castle was not used as a Prisoner-of-War camp in World War I.

Prisoners were inventive in devising methods to escape. They duplicated keys to various doors, made copies of maps, forged Ausweise (identity papers), and manufactured their own tools. MI9, a department of the British War Office which specialized in escape equipment, communicated with the prisoners in code and smuggled them new escape aids disguised in care packages from family or from non-existent charities, although they never tampered with Red Cross care packages for fear it would force the Germans to stop their delivery to all camps. The Germans became skilled at intercepting packages containing contraband material.

Prisoners also used items from their Red Cross parcels to buy information and tools from guards and local villagers

If a P.O.W. was lucky enough to escape from Colditz they would then face the considerable challenge of negotiating their way to a neutral country.

Dutch naval lieutenant Hans Larive discovered "The Singen Route" into Switzerland in 1940. On his first escape attempt Larive was caught near Singen, close to the Swiss border. The interrogating Gestapo officer was so confident the war would soon be won by Germany that he told Larive the safe way across the border. Larive did not forget and many prisoners later escaped using this route.

Most of the attempted escapes failed. Pat Reid, a British officer, failed to escape at first but then was appointed as "Escape Officer" in charge of coordinating the various escape groups. The Escape Officer would ensure escapes were controlled and not tripping over each other's attempts. Escape Officers were generally not permitted to escape while they held that position.

Many POWs tried unsuccessfully to escape in disguise: Airey Neave, a British officer, twice dressed as a guard and attempted to simply walk out A French Lieutenant, Boulé disguised himself as a woman. British Lieutenant Michael Sinclair even dressed as the German Sergeant Major

Rothenberger when he tried to organize a mass escape, and French Lieutenant Perodeau disguised as regular camp electrician Willi Pöhnert ("Little Willi"):

On the night of 28 December 1942, one of the French officers blew out the fuse on the lights in the courtyard. As they had anticipated Pöhnert was summoned, and while he was still fixing the lights, Lieutenant Perodeau, dressed almost identically to Pöhnert and carrying a tool box, walked casually out of the courtyard gate. He passed the first guard without incident, but the guard at the main gate asked for his token — tokens were issued to each guard and staff member upon entry of the camp guardhouse specifically to avoid this type of escape — with no hope of bluffing his way out of this, Perodeau surrendered.

Dutch sculptors made two clay heads to stand in for escaping officers in the roll call. Later, "ghosts", officers who had faked a successful escape and hid in the castle, took the place of escaping prisoners in the roll call in order to delay discovery as long as possible.

Camp guards collected so much escape equipment that they established a "Commandant's Escape Museum". Local photographer Johannes Lange took photographs of the would-be escapers in their disguises or re-enacting their attempts for the camera. Along with the Lange photographs, one of the two sculpted clay heads was displayed proudly in the museum.

There was only one confirmed fatality during the escape attempts: British Lieutenant Michael Sinclair in September 1944. Sinclair attempted a repeat of the 1941 French over the wire escape. Security officer Eggers warned him after which Sinclair was fired upon by guards. A bullet hit Sinclair on the elbow and ricocheted through his heart.

The Germans buried him in Colditz cemetery with full military honours — his casket was draped with a Union Jack flag made by the German guards, and he received a seven-gun salute. Post-war he was awarded the Distinguished Service Order, the only man to receive it for escaping during World War II. He is currently buried in grave number 10.1.14 at Berlin War Cemetery in the Charlottenburg-Wilmersdorf district of Berlin.

Flight Lieutenant Dominic Bruce was a tiny-framed individual. He arrived at Colditz in 1942 after attempting to escape from Spangenberg Castle disguised as a Red Cross doctor. A new Commandant arrived at Colditz in the summer of 1942; he enforced rules restricting prisoners' personal belongings. On 8 September POWs were told to pack up all excess belongings and an assortment of boxes were delivered to carry them into store. Dominic Bruce immediately seized his chance and was packed inside a Red Cross packing case, three-foot square, with just a file and a forty-foot length rope made of bed sheets. Bruce was taken to a storeroom on the third floor of the German Kommandantur and made his escape that night. When the German guards discovered the bed rope dangling from the window the following morning they raced to the storeroom and found the empty box. Bruce had inscribed 'Die Luft in Colditz gefällt mir nicht mehr. Auf Wiedersehen'! — "The air in Colditz no longer agrees with me. See you later!"

Bruce was recaptured a week later trying to stow aboard a Swedish ship in Danzig.

**Bruce's Escape Box**

In late 1940, British officer Peter Allan found out that the Germans were moving several mattresses from the castle to another camp and decided that would be his way out. He let the French officers moving the mattresses know that one would be a little bit heavier. Allan, a fluent German speaker, dressed himself up in a Hitlerjugend (Hitler Youth) uniform, stuffed Reichsmark in his pockets, and had himself sewn into one of the mattresses. He managed to get himself loaded into the truck, and unloaded into an empty house within the town. Cutting himself out of the mattress several hours later when there was complete silence he climbed out of the window and into the garden and swaggered down the road towards his freedom.

Making his way to Vienna one hundred and sixty kilometres down the road via Stuttgart he got a lift with a senior SS officer. Allan recalled that ride as the scariest moment of his life. He had been aiming to reach Poland but soon after reaching Vienna found his money had run out.

America had not yet entered the war so Allan decided to ask the American consulate for assistance; he was refused. His stepmother, Lois Allan, was a U.S. citizen he was sure the embassy would take him in. Allan had been on the run at this point for nine days; broke, exhausted, and hungry, he fell asleep in a park. Upon waking he discovered he was too weak to walk. Soon after he was picked up and returned to Colditz, where he spent the next three months in solitary confinement.

On 12 May 1941, Polish Lieutenants Miki Surmanowicz and Mietek Chmiel attempted to rappel down a thirty-six meter wall to freedom on a rope constructed out of bed sheets. In order to get into a suitable position both men orchestrated punishment in solitary confinement. After forcing open the door and picking the locks they made their way to the courtyard where they climbed up to a narrow ledge. From the ledge they were able to cross to the guardhouse roof, and climb through an open window on the outer wall. Utilising their bed sheet rope, they lowered themselves towards the ground. Both were caught when the German guards heard the hobnailed boots of one of the escapees scraping down the outside of the guardhouse wall. The guard who spotted the escapees shouted 'Hände hoch!!' [Hands up!!] to the men as they were descending the rope. As if.

## Audacious Escapes

### Female Impersonator

On June 5 1941, while returning from the park to the castle, some British prisoners noticed that a passing lady dropped her watch. One of the British POWs called out to her, but the lady just kept walking. This aroused the suspicion of the German guards and, upon inspection, "she" was revealed to be a French officer – Lieutenant Chasseurs Alpins Bouley.

### The Canteen Tunnel

Early in 1941, the British prisoners had gained access to the sewers and drains, which ran beneath the floors of the castle. Entrance to these was from a manhole cover in the floor of the canteen. After initial reconnaissance trips it was decided that the drain should be extended and an exit made in a small grassy area, which was overlooked from the canteen window. From there they planned to climb down the hill and drop below the steep outside eastern wall of the castle. The escapees knew which sentry would be on duty during the night of the escape, they pooled their resources and collected 500 Reichsmark for a bribe. This plan took three months to prepare. On the evening of 29 May 1941, Pat Reid hid in the canteen after it had been locked up for the night. Having removed the bolt from the lock on the door, he returned to the courtyard. After evening roll call the escapers slipped into the canteen unnoticed. They entered the tunnel and waited for the signal to proceed. Unknown to the prisoners, they had been betrayed by the bribed guard. Waiting on the grassy area to greet them was Hauptmann Priem, the commandant and his guard force.

Pat Reid recalls:

> *"I climbed out on to the grass and Rupert Barry was following close behind. My shadow was cast on the wall of the Kommandantur, and at that moment I noticed a second shadow beside my own. It held a gun. I yelled to Rupert to get back as a voice behind me shouted, Hände hoch! Hände hoch!. I turned to face a German officer levelling his pistol at me."*

Behind him were seven British and four Polish officers. On his order the remaining men backed up the tunnel to evade detection but the Germans were waiting for them outside the canteen. Not wanting to give their captors any satisfaction the British burst into laughter as they came out.

Hauptmann Priem ends the story:

"And the Guard? He kept his 100 Marks; he got extra leave, promotion and the War Service Cross."


## The French Tunnel

Nine French officers organised a long-term tunnel-digging project, the longest attempted out of Colditz Castle throughout the war. Deciding that the exit should be on the steep drop leading down towards the recreation area, outside the eastern walls of the castle. The officers began to scout for a possible location for the entrance. Lieutenants Cazaumayo and Paille had previously gained access to the clock tower in 1940. Both officers knew how to solve the problem.

Their tunnel began at the top of the chapel's clock tower and descended nearly nine meters into the ground using the shaft containing the ropes and weights for the clock. They discovered the weights and chains had been removed. This left an empty shaft, which extended from the clock to the cellars below. After the 1940 escape attempt by Cazaumayo and

Paille the doors, which provided access to the tower, had been bricked up in order to prevent further attempts. However, by sealing up the tower the Germans had in essence provided a secure location. Now work could be done without being noticed. The French gained access to the tower from the attic and descended thirty-five meters to the cellars. Work began on a horizontal shaft in June 1941. This shaft work would continue for a further eight months.

The horizontal shaft towards the chapel progressed four meters before they hit rock the decision was taken to dig upwards towards the chapel floor. From here the tunnel continued underneath the wooden floor of the chapel for a distance of thirteen and a half meters. For this to be achieved, seven heavy oak timbers in the floor had to be cut through. Homemade saws assembled from table knives were employed for this task. Once completed, the tunnel dropped vertically from the far corner of the chapel a further five meters. The tunnel then proceeded out towards the proposed exit with two further descents separated by shafts in the stone foundations of the castle. The tunnel now ran a horizontal distance of forty-four meters reaching a final depth of eight and a half meters below the surface.

Tunnelling continued well into 1942. By then Germans knew that the French were digging somewhere, based on the noise of their digging reverberating through the castle at night. The French thought the tunnel's entrance was undetectable. However, on 15 January the Germans eventually searched the clock tower. Noise was heard below, and after lowering a small boy down the shaft three French officers were found. After searching the cellar thoroughly the entrance to the tunnel was eventually discovered a mere two meters short of completion. The French officers were convinced they had been betrayed by one of their own countrymen but this was never proven.

The tunnel had electric lighting along its whole length, powered by electricity from the chapel. Five large stones covering a small door, which left little trace of any hole, concealed the entrance to the tunnel in the wine cellar

**The "Colditz Cock" glider**

One of the most ambitious and imaginative escape attempts from Colditz was the idea of building a glider and flying to freedom. The idea came from two British pilots, Jack Best and Bill Goldfinch. Two army officers, Tony Rolt and David Walker who had recently arrived in the camp, encouraged them. It would be Tony Rolt who would recommend the chapel roof; he noticed it was obscured from the view of the Germans.

The two-man glider was to be assembled by the two pilots in the lower attic above the chapel it was to be launched from the roof to give it the elevation to fly across the river Mulde which was about sixty meters below. The runway was constructed from tables and the glider was to be launched using a pulley system based on a falling metal bathtub full of concrete, which would accelerate the glider to fifty kilometres an hour.

Prisoners built a false wall to hide the space in the attic where they slowly built the glider out of stolen wood. The Germans were incensed on discovering tunnels not secret workshops therefore the prisoners felt safe from detection. However, they still placed lookouts and created an electric alarm system to warn the builders of approaching guards.

Hundreds of ribs for the fuselage had to be constructed; they smuggled in timber predominantly from bed slats but also from every other piece of wood the POW's could obtain. The wing spars were constructed from floorboards. Control wires were made from electrical wiring taken from unused portions of the castle. A glider expert, Lorne Welch, reviewed the stress diagrams and calculations made by Goldfinch.

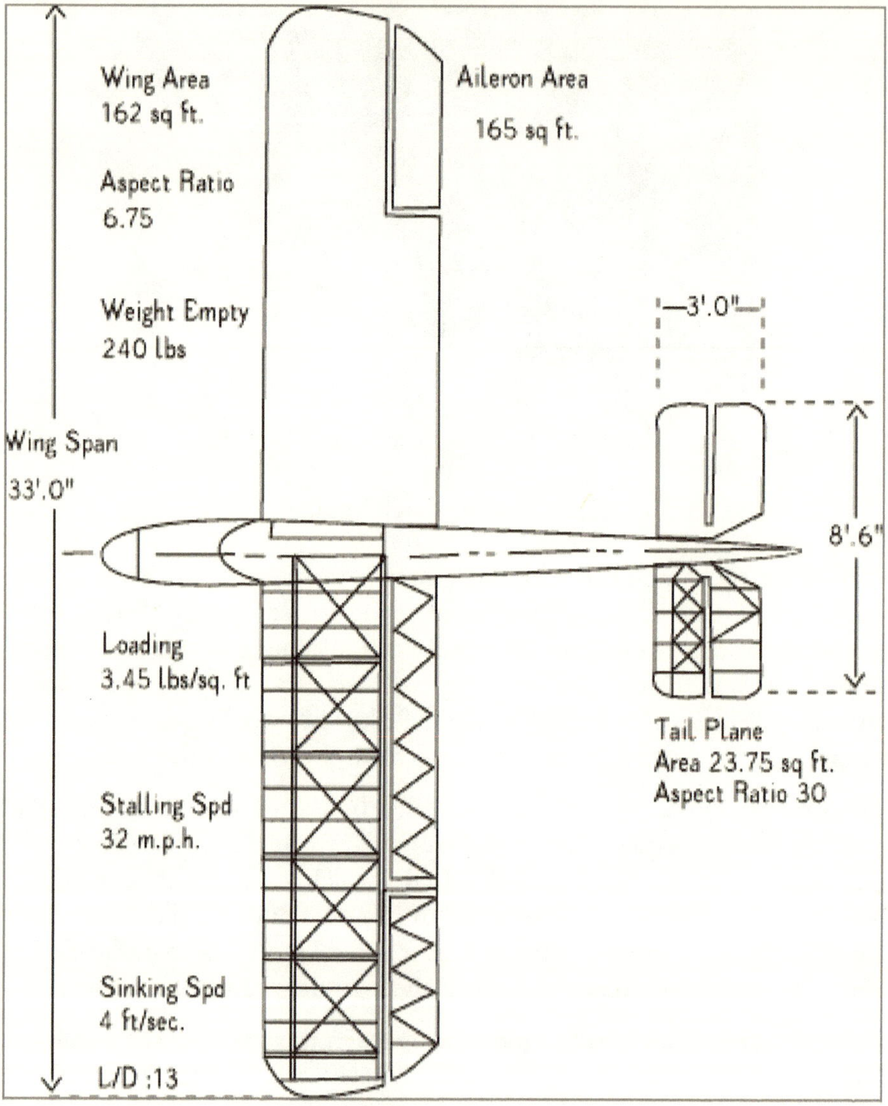

Wing Area
162 sq ft.

Aileron Area
165 sq ft.

Aspect Ratio
6.75

Weight Empty
240 lbs

⊢—3'.0"—⊣

Wing Span
33'.0"

8'.6"

Loading
3.45 lbs/sq. ft

Tail Plane
Area 23.75 sq ft.
Aspect Ratio 30

Stalling Spd
32 m.p.h.

Sinking Spd
4 ft/sec.

L/D :13

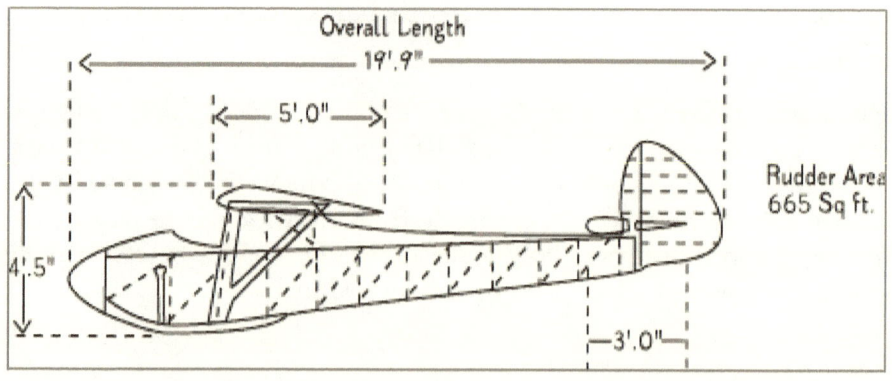

Overall Length
19'.9"

5'.0"

Rudder Area
665 Sq ft.

4'.5"

3'.0"

The resulting glider was to be a one hundred and nine kilograms two-seater, high wing, monoplane design. It had a Mooney style rudder and square elevators. The wingspan was thirty-three feet and the fuselage length was nineteen feet. Prison sleeping bags of blue and white checked cotton were used to provide the skin for the glider. German ration millet was boiled and used to seal the cloth pores.

The war ended before the glider was finished.

It was flown for a film on Colditz and it was a successful flight.

## Tools Created for the Construction

*Side-framed saw*

*handle of beech bed board*

*frame of iron window bars*

*blade of gramophone spring with 8 teeth / in (3 mm teeth)*

*Minute saw for fine work*

*gramophone spring blade, 25 teeth / in (1 mm teeth)*

*5/8 in (16 mm) metal drill obtained by bribery*

*Drill bits for making holes made from nails*

*A gauge made of beech, with cupboard bolt and gramophone needle*

*Large plane, 14½ in (368 mm) long*

**Home Made Plane**

*2 inch blade obtained by bribing a German guard*

*Wooden box (four pieces of beech screwed together)*

*Small plane, 8½ in (216 mm) long blade made from a table knife*

*Plane, 5 in (127 mm) long*

*Square made of beech with gramophone spring blade*

*Set of keys including:*

*Universal door pick, forged from a bucket handle*

# FRENCH LETTERS

## CHAPTER 18

General Henri Giraud, a French Commander, was a celebrated warrior who had served in North Africa prior to World War One. He graduated from the Saint-Cyr Military Academy in 1900 and joined the French Army, commanding Zouave troops in North Africa until he was transferred back to France in 1914 when World War I broke out.

It was during World War One that Giraud was seriously wounded while serving as a captain. Giraud commanded a Battalion of Zouaves. In their day the Zouaves were better known than the French Foreign Legion, revered by their countrymen as tough, dashing, roistering daredevils -- the heroes of many a hard-fought battle, and the stuff of legend.

He was leading a bayonet charge during the Battle of Charleroi on 21 August 1914 when he was seriously wounded and left for dead on the battlefield. He was captured by the Germans and placed in a prison camp in Belgium. He managed to escape two months later by pretending to be a roustabout with a traveling circus. He then asked Edith Cavell for help, and eventually he was able to return to France via the Netherlands.

Edith Cavell was a British nurse. She is celebrated for saving the lives of soldiers from both sides without discrimination and in helping some two hundred Allied soldiers escape from German-occupied Belgium during the First World War, for which she was arrested. She was subsequently court-martialled, found guilty of treason and sentenced to death. Despite international pressure for mercy, she was shot by a German firing squad. Her execution received worldwide condemnation and extensive press coverage.

Once the end of the war was declared on the 11th November 1918 Giraud served with French troops in Constantinople under General Franchet d'Esperey. In 1933, he was transferred to Morocco to fight against Rif (kabyle) rebels. He was awarded the *Légion d'Honneur* after the capture of Abd-el-Krim and later became the military commander of Metz. He also taught military strategy at the École de Guerre, where one of his students was Captain Charles de Gaulle.

## 1940

When World War II began, Giraud became a member of the Superior War Council along with Charles de Gaulle, with whom he disagreed about the tactics of using armoured troops. He became the commander of the 7th Army when it was sent to the Netherlands on 10 May 1940 and was able to delay German troops at Breda on 13 May. As a consequence, many casualties occurred requiring the merger of the 7th Army with the 9th. Giraud was a General who led from the front; he was riding in a Jeep on a reconnaissance patrol when the Germans captured him; he had been trying to block a German attack through the Ardennes. A court-martial tried Giraud for ordering the execution of two German saboteurs wearing civilian clothes, but he was acquitted and taken to Königstein Castle near Dresden, which was used as a high-security POW prison.

Giraud planned his escape carefully over the following two years. He taught himself German and memorised a map of the surrounding area. He made a one hundred and fifty foot rope out of twine, torn bed sheets, and copper wire, which friends had smuggled, into the prison for him. Using a simple code embedded in his letters home, he informed his family of his plans to escape. On 17 April 1942, he lowered himself down the cliff of the mountain fortress. He had shaved off his moustache, and, donned a Tyrolean hat so he looked like a typical German local. Henri travelled to Schandau to meet his Special Operations Executive contact who provided him with a change of clothes, cash and identity papers. Through various ruses, he reached the Swiss border by train. To avoid border guards he trekked through the mountains until he was apprehended by two Swiss soldiers, who took him to Basle.

Giraud eventually made it into Vichy France, where he revealed his identity. He tried to convince Marshal Pétain that Germany could be beaten, and that France must resist the German occupation. His views were rejected, but the Vichy government refused to return Giraud to the Germans.

Safely in his beloved France, he was lauded by the French people for his escape, which gave them faith that the Germans would be ultimately defeated. Hitler was furious and ordered his capture and execution; he survived an assassination attempt in August 1944.

In November 1944 Giraud was taken by submarine from Gibraltar to meet with General Eisenhower to discuss his role in the Allied invasion. One condition he insisted on was that the French troops would support the American troops, not the British. He had a deep-seated mistrust of his cousins across the channel. He also demanded that he lead the invasion, a condition to which Eisenhower could not agree. Giraud eventually agreed to serve under Vichy Admiral Francois Darlan who had the support of both Eisenhower and Churchill. Darlan was assassinated on 24 December 1942, giving Giraud the opportunity to lead the French troops.

Giraud served as co-president of the French Committee of National Liberation with Charles de Gaulle. This was not a partnership that could be sustained and eventually de Gaulle forced him out. He retired in 1944 and died in 1949.

**Giraud, (left) Roosevelt, de Gaulle and Churchill
at the Casablanca Conference January 1943**

# GERMANY TO VIETNAM

## CHAPTER 19

Dieter Dengler was born May 22, 1938 and grew up in the small town of Wildberg, in the Black Forest region of the German state of Baden-WurttembergDieter never knew his father he had been killed in the Second World War; nevertheless he had a good family life despite the poor living conditions they all had to endure.

Dieter was very close to his Mother and brothers and they all worked together to survive life in post war Germany.

His grandfather was an avid opponent of Hitler's National Socialism and showed great strength in not voting for the Nazis in the elections. Dieter credited his grandfather's resolve in being the inspiration he needed in later life.

Dieter's first experience with aircraft was when he witnessed Allied aircraft bombing his hometown. From that moment, he wanted to be a pilot.

He grew up in extreme poverty, as a result he and his brothers discovered ways to keep the family fed and sheltered. They would go into bombed-out buildings, tear off wallpaper, and bring it to his mother to boil for a meal. Apparently, some nutrients remained in the wallpaper paste. When the Moroccans, who occupied the area, would slaughter sheep for their meals, Dieter would sneak over to their lodgings to take the scraps and parts they wouldn't eat. His mother was very inventive in the ways she could make a tasty meal. Dieter was also the first in his town to have a bicycle, building it himself by scavenging from dumps. He was apprenticed to a blacksmith at the age of fourteen, the blacksmith was a very hard taskmaster and beatings were a regular occurrence. Later in life, Dieter actually acknowledged his master for his disciplined training; it helped him become more capable, self-reliant, and tough enough to survive almost anything.

After seeing a recruitment advertisement in an American magazine looking for pilots, he decided to go to the United States.

The one thing that stopped him from going was lack of funds, he had to find a way to earn enough money to pay for his passage. He decided to salvage brass and other metals and sell them on the open market. This venture proved to be very successful and by the time he turned eighteen he had saved enough to sail to America.

Dieter made his way to Hamburg by hitching rides and walking departing for America and a new life. His final port was New York, a city that filled him with wonderment and awe.

He had nowhere to stay so he made the streets of Manhattan his home until he discovered the Air Force recruitment centre he applied and was accepted into the air force in 1957. Dieter was excited about the prospect of becoming a fighter pilot his lifetime ambition. He attended basic training in Texas and was assigned to work as a motor mechanic in the motor pool, hardly a dream fulfilled.

He took and passed the test to become an aviation cadet but his enlistment expired before he was selected for pilot training.

After his discharge, Dieter joined his brother working in a bakery shop near San Francisco he enrolled in the San Francisco City College passing his final year exams he then transferred to the College of San Mateo where he studied aeronautics. After graduating from college two years of college, he applied for the US Navy aviation cadet program and was accepted.

Dieter was determined to become a pilot. In his inaugural flight at flight training the instructor told Dieter that if he became airsick and vomited in the cockpit, he would receive a "down" on his record. He knew he was only allowed three downs before he received a fail. As Dieter expected, the instructor took the plane through spins and loops, causing Dieter to become dizzy and disoriented. Knowing he was about to vomit and not wanting to receive a down, Dieter took off his boot, threw up into it, and put it back on. At the end of the flight, the instructor checked the cockpit but couldn't find any evidence of vomit. Dieter still had a clean slate.

After his completion of flight training, he was assigned to Naval Air Station Corpus Christi, Texas for training to become an attack pilot in the Douglas AD Skyraider.

**Douglas AD Skyraider**

He joined his squadron, VA-145 while they were on shore duty at Naval Air Station Alameda, California. In 1965 the squadron joined the carrier *USS Ranger*

In December the carrier set sail for the coast of Vietnam. He was stationed initially at **Dixie Station** off South Vietnam, and then moved north to **Yankee Station** for operations against North Vietnam. Life was about to change for Dieter.

# WELCOME TO THE HANOI HILTON

## CHAPTER 20

On February 1, 1966, the day after the carrier *Ranger* began flying missions from Yankee Station, Lieutenant Junior Dengler launched from the carrier with three other aircraft on an interdiction mission against a truck convoy that had been reported leaving North Vietnam. Thunderstorms forced the pilots to divert to their secondary target, a road intersection located west of the Mu Gia Pass in Laos. At the time, U.S. air operations in Laos were classified "secret." Visibility was poor due to smoke plumes emanating from burning fields. The flight formation lost site of each other Dengler was hit by anti-aircraft fire.

'There was a large explosion on my right side.' He remembered

'The airplane seemed to cartwheel through the sky in slow motion. There were more explosions yet, I was still able to guide the plane into a clearing in Laos.

Many times, people have asked me if I was afraid. Just before dying, there is no more fear. I felt I was floating.'

Thrown over thirty metres from the plane in a crash-landing, Dengler lay unconscious for a few minutes before making his way into the jungle to hide.

His squadron leader hoped to God that the young pilot would be rescued.

Dieter had earned himself a tough reputation while attending the navy survival school. He had escaped from a mock-POW camp run by SERE instructors and Marine guards twice, he had also set a record as the only student to actually gain weight during the course. His childhood experiences enabled him to eat whatever he could scavenge including the scraps the course instructors threw in the garbage.

Dieter's radio and survival kit were destroyed as a result of the crash landing; he really was on his own in enemy territory.

He only lasted a day before being discovered by the Pathet Lao, the Laotian allies of the Viet Cong.

He knew life was not going to be easy from then on; they tied his hands and marched him through the dense jungle

At night, he was tied spread-eagled on the ground to four stakes this not only prohibited him from escaping it prohibited him from getting any sleep. In the mornings, his face would be so swollen from mosquito bites he was unable to see clearly

He took an opportunity to escape into the jungle but it was a short-lived freedom, he was recaptured and subjected to a range of tortures.

He was hung upside down by his ankles with a nest of fierce ants covering his face eventually he would lose consciousness.

At night, they suspended him in a freezing well, he knew if he fell asleep he would drown.

Other times, he was dragged by water buffalo through villages, his guards laughing as they goaded both he and the animal with a whip.

Bloodied and almost broken, he was asked by Pathet Lao officers to sign a document condemning America, he refused, so the torture intensified. Tiny wedges of bamboo were inserted under his fingernails and into incisions on his body to grow and fester.

After some weeks, Dengler was handed over to the Viet Cong. As they marched him through a village, a man slipped Dieters's engagement ring from his finger. He complained to his guards. They found the culprit, summarily chopped off his finger with a machete and threw the finger aside once the ring was retrieved. Dieter was horrified. 'I realised right there and then that you didn't fool around with the Viet Cong. He said.

Dengler was eventually brought to a prison camp near the village of Par Kung where he met several other POWs.

They were:

> *Pisidhi Indradat (Thai)*
>
> *Prasit Promsuwan (Thai)*
>
> *Prasit Thanee (Thai)*
>
> *Y.C. To (Chinese)*
>
> *Duane W. Martin (American)*
>
> *Eugene DeBruin (American)*

Apart for Martin, an air force helicopter pilot who had been shot down in North Vietnam nearly a year before, the other prisoners were civilians employed by Air America, a civilian airline owned by the Central Intelligence Agency. The civilians had been in Pathet Lao hands for over two and a half years when Dengler joined them.

He had hoped he would be joining a group of pilots all plotting an escape; a bit like Douglas Bader and his comrades in World War Two.

What he saw horrified him, there was one man carrying his intestines cupped in his hands another had barely any teeth left, the few he had were badly ulcerated and extremely painful. He begged the other POWs to knock them out with a rock.

All the prisoners were in very bad shape Dieter knew he had to escape or he would end up like these poor fellows inside six months. He informed the other prisoners his intention to escape on his first day in the camp. They all suggested he wait until the monsoon season arrived ensuring he would always have access to fresh water. A few weeks after Dieter had arrived in the camp the Viet Cong moved them all to another camp just twenty kilometres away at Hoi Het.

The group split into camps, those who wanted to escape including Dieter, Martin and Prasit the others were opposed.

The food available became less and less the daily ration consisted of a cup of rice to be shared by all of them. The POWs occasionally caught a snake or a rat, which would be devoured by the prisoners; it was the only meat they could get.

Sleeping at night was difficult; the men were shackled together with their feet locked in foot blocks. They couldn't move, and together with the chronic dysentery most of them suffered they were forced to lie in their own excrement until being released in the morning.

Prasit Promsuwan, a Thai prisoner, overheard two guards discussing a plan to take the prisoners into the jungle and shoot them all. They were planning to make it look like an escape attempt then they could return home to their villages.

Prasit informed the other POWs as to what he had heard Dieter, was determined that he and the other men should escape as soon as possible. They lie bound in their shackles that night and devised a plan. At lunchtime the guards would lay down their weapons; this and the evening meal were the only times the guards were not armed. They agreed midday would be the best time to enact the plan so they could see their way when they entered the jungle. Dieter and another prisoner loosened the floorboards, which would enable them to squeeze through. The plan was to rush the guards seize their weapons and disappear into the jungle.

# The Escape

## June 26 1966

The group managed to break out of their manacles using sharpened bamboo to pick the locks the same method was used to free their feet. They all squeezed out between the floorboards and lay in wait for the guards to begin their lunch of rice and deer. They made their move running about five metres and grabbed the weapons including a M1 rifle Chinese automatic rifles and a sub machine gun. Dieter grabbed a AK47 just as five of the guards rushed him, he manage to shoot and kill three the other two escaped into the jungle

The seven prisoners split into three groups. DeBruin was originally supposed to go with Dieter and Martin however he decided to be with To to support his Chinese friend who was recovering from a fever and would be unable to keep up. They intended to get over the nearest ridge and wait for rescue. Dieter and Duane Martin decided to head for the Mekong River enabling them to escape to Thailand.

At last the two the two American airmen were free from the horrors of their camp however escape brought its own torments. Soon, the two men's feet were white and mangled from trekking through the dense jungle. This was similar to what the soldiers in the trenches during World War One called "trench feet".

They found the sole of an old tennis shoe, which they took turns wearing, strapping it onto a foot with rattan for a few hours respite.

They were able to make their way to a fast-flowing river.

'It was the highway to freedom.' Said Dengler,

'We knew it would flow into the Mekong River, which would take us over the border into Thailand and safety.'

The men built a raft from logs tied together with rattan and floated downstream encountering ferocious rapids along he way. At night they would tie the raft to a solid tree on the riverbank ensuring the raft wasn't swept away by the fast lowing torrent. He would wake to be greeted by hundreds of leeches sucking their much needed blood.

Dieter observed villages which looked familiar he was sure they had passed them days before; they had been going around in a circle this river would not take them to the Mekong and freedom.

They set up camp in an abandoned village where they found shelter from the incessant rain. Although Dieter and Duane had brought rice with them and were able to find other food they were still on the verge of starvation.

The two escapees were hoping to send a signal to an American C-130 which they had seen crossing over the village on a regular basis. Using the gunpowder from some carbine cartridges they had kept dry they were able to light a fire. They created torches from bamboo and bracken, they waved them when the C-130 flew above the village. To their delight the plane circled and dropped a couple of flares. They went to sleep that night feeling confident that a rescue mission would free them next morning. No such rescue happened.

When, next morning, they realised there would be no rescue both Dieter and Duane felt totally demoralised.

Duane convinced Dieter it was worth the risk to approach a nearby village, Akha to see if they could obtain some food. Dieter was reluctant but he would not abandon his friend, he agreed to go.

They entered the village and saw a young boy playing stick with his dog, the two men approached him smiling and holding out their hands. The boy turned and ran back to his home yelling "AMERICAN'. A male villager appeared almost immediately Dieter and Duane knelt down in supplication. The man swung a machete he was holding hitting Duane in the leg he struck again and Duane was decapitated.

Dieter quickly rose to his feet rushed towards the villager who turned and ran back into the village losing his rubber thongs in his mad rush to get help. Dieter picked up the thongs and ran back into the jungle before the other villagers confronted him.

The only highlight of his time in the jungle was befriending a bear it became his substitute dog following him wherever he went. It helped Dieter keep his sanity.

He was alone, staving and floating in and out of a hallucinatory state, he had little confidence that he would ever be rescued but he never gave up trying.

Dieter managed to evade the searchers who were searching for him escaping back into the jungle. He returned to the abandoned village that night when a C-130 came over Dieter set fire to the huts and burned the village down. The C-130 crew spotted the fires and dropped flares, but even though the crew reported their sighting when they returned to their base at Ubon, Thailand, the fires were not recognized by intelligence as having been a signal from a survivor.

When a rescue force again failed to materialize, Dieter decided to try and find one of the parachutes from a flare for use as a possible signal. He found one on a bush and placed it in his rucksack.

On July 20, 1966, after twenty-three days in the jungle, Dengler managed to signal an Air Force pilot with the parachute. Air Force Skyraiders from the 1st Air Commando Squadron happened to fly up the river where Dengler was located. Eugene Deatrick, the pilot of the lead plane and the squadron commander, spotted a flash of white while making a turn at the river's bend and came back and spotted a man waving something white. Deatrick and his wingman contacted rescue forces but were told to ignore the sighting, as no airmen were known to be down in the area. Deatrick persisted and eventually managed to convince the command and control centre to dispatch a rescue force. Fearing that Dengler might be a Viet Cong soldier, the helicopter crew restrained him when he was brought aboard.

Air Force Para-rescue specialist Michael Leonard stripped Dieter of his clothes, making sure he was not armed or in possession of a hand grenade. When questioned, Dieter told Leonard that he had escaped from a North Vietnamese POW camp two months earlier. Deatrick radioed the rescue helicopter crew to see if they could identify the person they had just hoisted up from the jungle. They reported that they had a man who claimed to be a downed Navy pilot who flew a Douglas A-1H Skyraider.

It wasn't until after he reached the hospital at Da Nang that Dieter's identity was confirmed. A dispute between the Air Force and the Navy developed over who should conduct his debriefing and recovery. In an apparent attempt to prevent the Air Force from embarrassing them in some way, the Navy sent a team of SEALs into the hospital to literally steal Dieter. He was brought out of the hospital in a covered gurney and rushed to the airfield, where he was placed aboard a Navy carrier delivery transport and flown to the *Ranger* where a welcoming party had been prepared. At night, however, he was tormented by awful dreams and had to be restrained.

Dieter's condition was such that the Navy decided to fly him back to the United States for treatment.

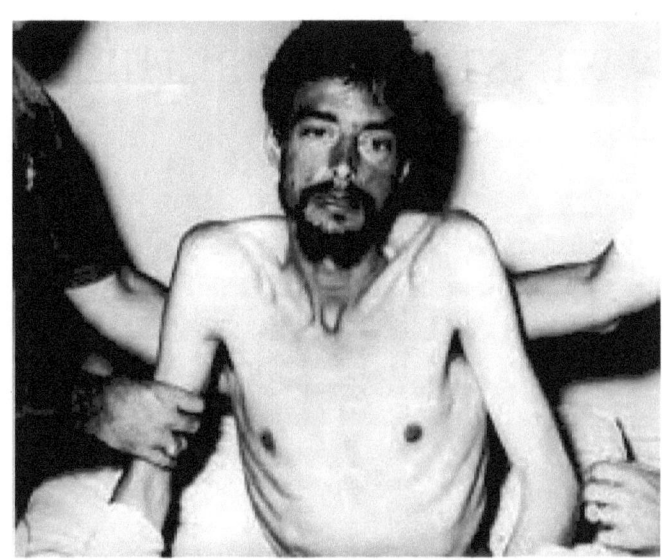

**Photo taken of Dengler in the hospital after his rescue.**

**At 175 cm Dengler weighed only 44.45 kilos.**

'Seven of us escaped,' said Dengler. 'I was the only one who came out alive.'

With the exception of Indradat, who was recaptured and later rescued by Laotian troops, none of the other prisoners were ever seen again.

# WINSTON CHURCHILL

## CHAPTER 21

In 1895, Winston Churchill, a 2nd Lieutenant, 4th Queen's Own Hussars, began to take an interest in war correspondence in an effort to supplement the income he was receiving from his regiment. It was never his intention nor ambition to follow a conventional Army career but rather to seek out all possible chances of military action, using his mother's and family's influence in high society to arrange postings to active campaigns. He became a war correspondent for several London newspapers and wrote books about the campaigns.

On the 11 October 1899, the Second Boer War between Britain and the Boer Republics broke out. Churchill obtained a commission to act as war correspondent for *The Morning Post* with a salary of £250 per month. He accepted an invitation to accompany the 17th Lancers known as "Death or Glory Lads" on a raid against the Boers at Elandslaagte.

Winston and the Lancers were travelling on an armoured train, performing a reconnoitre between Frere and Chieveley in the British Natal Colony in November 1899. A Boer commando force had placed a big boulder on the track; the train rounded a bend, smashing into it. The locomotive derailed and the Boers opened up with field guns and rifle fire from various positions.

Those British soldiers who were uninjured returned fire, whilst others on the train did their best to get the injured and wounded out of harm's way.

Although the carriages had derailed, the locomotive remained on the track. The soldiers attempted to uncouple the train, hoping to reverse back down the track however the incessant fire from the Boers made this a difficult task. Eventually the Boers swept down the hillside and captured the train and its occupants; a number of men were taken prisoner. Eventually the locomotive with some of the men escaped. Churchill found himself alone in a gully near the track. It was summer and the heat was stifling; he was covered in sweat, oil and dirt and was exhausted. A Boer officer dismounted from his horse, got down on one knee and raised his Mauser rifle. Churchill reached for the pistol and found his holster empty: he'd lost it on the train. He was defenceless and had no choice but to surrender.

The Boer officer took the young Winston into custody but what neither of them realised at the time was their destinies would cross again. Both these men would become prime ministers of their respective countries! Ironically their countries would fight in another war as allies in a few short years The Boer commander was General Louis Botha.

General Louis Botha

Churchill was a nondescript twenty- five year old at the time but was a member of an elite British family. His father, Lord Randolph Churchill, had been an eminent politician and the family bloodline went back to beyond the First Duke of Marlborough. The Boers knew they had a valuable prisoner who could be used in future negotiations with the British. The Boers, for many reasons, decided to treat Winston as a POW, despite the fact he was a civilian.

**Winston Standing on the Right of Other British Prisoners**

The prisoners were marched for some miles in the scorching heat before being loaded on a train heading for Pretoria. Along the way, they passed an imposing mountain, a mountain the British would rather forget, "Majuba Hill" came into view. Winston, however, remembered the mountain well it was here in February 1881, the Boers defeated the British army using their hit- and- run guerrilla warfare tactics. Soon after that humiliating defeat, the British negotiated a ceasefire thus ending the first Anglo-Boer War. This act of obtaining a ceasefire was described by the young Churchill as 'a disgraceful, cowardly peace.' After the Battle of Majuba, the British army never again wore their famous red tunics into battle; they adopted khaki combat uniforms thereafter.

**Majuba Hill**

**British in Khaki**

When the train transporting the prisoners passed by Majuba it was early evening and the light was fading. Churchill described the sight as 'a great dark mountain with memories as sad and gloomy as its appearance'.

The prisoners' train then continued on its journey to Pretoria

'I rode on home from Volksrust across the monotonous veld. Eventually the oh-so-familiar sight of Johannesburg's skyline about 15 miles away came into view, silhouetted against the late afternoon sun, signalling the end of another trip.'

Churchill and his colleagues were imprisoned in a converted school in the middle of Pretoria.

The prisoners were marched through the streets of Pretoria, reaching the prison school in the late afternoon. Churchill's observations on first sight of the State Model Schools building were:

'We turned a corner; on the other side of the road stood a long, low, red brick building with a slated veranda and a row of iron railings before it.'

Churchill decided quickly that captivity was not for him, thus he began to plot his escape on the first night at the prison school. On the night of December 12th, when several prison guards had turned their backs, he took the opportunity to climb over the prison wall. Wearing a brown flannel suit with £75 in his pocket and four slabs of chocolate, Churchill walked leisurely on through the night, in the hope of finding the Delagoa Bay Railway. So began his great escape and journey to freedom.

Churchill jumped onto a train and hid among soft sacks covered in coal dust. Leaving the train before daybreak, he continued on his escape. Lady luck was on his side, when Winston happened upon the home of Mr John Howard, manager of the Transvaal Collieries. He knocked on the front door; Mr Howard's response to his plea for help was 'Thank God you have come here! It is the only house for twenty miles where you would not have been handed over. We are all British here, we will see you through.'

Mr Howard first hid Churchill in a coalmine, which made the young Winston quite ill, after which, Mr Howard transported him to safety. Churchill had to squeeze into a hole at the end of a train car loaded with bales of wool. This was a very uncomfortable journey.

Once he arrived in Durban, a British stronghold, he was hailed as a hero.

# OTHER SUCCESSFUL ESCAPE ATTEMPTS

It is claimed that there were thirty-six "home runs" i.e. successful escapes from Colditz.

At the end of May 1943, the Armed Forces High Command decided that Colditz should hold only British and Commonwealth officers As a result all of the Dutch and Polish prisoners and most of the French and Belgians were moved to other camps in July. Three British officers tried their luck by impersonating French officers when they were moved out but they were later returned to Colditz. German security gradually improved and by the end of 1943 most of the potential avenues of escape had been eliminated. Several officers tried to escape during transit without success.

Some officers faked illnesses including mental illness in order to be repatriated on medical grounds. A member of the Royal Army Medical Corps (RAMC), Captain Ion Ferguson wrote a letter to an Irish friend suggesting Ireland join the war; the censors stopped the letter but his wish to be moved elsewhere was granted.. Four other British officers claimed symptoms of stomach ulcer, insanity, high blood pressure and back injury in order to be repatriated. However, there were also officers who went genuinely insane.

French Lieutenant Alain Le Ray escaped April 11, 1941. He hid in a terrace house in a park during a game of football. He was the first successful Colditz escaper and the first to reach neutral Switzerland.

French Lieutenant René Collin escaped May 31, 1941. He climbed into the rafters of a pavilion during exercise hiding there until dark he slipped away. He made it back to France.

French Lieutenant Pierre Mairesse Lebrun escaped July 2, 1941. He was captured. At a later date he vaulted over a wire fence in a park with the help of an associate. He reached Switzerland in eight days on a stolen bicycle.

Dutch Lieutenant Hans Larive escaped August 15, 1941. He hid under a manhole cover in the exercise enclosure emerging after nightfall Hans took a train to Gottmadingen reaching Switzerland in three days.

British Lieutenant Airey M. S. Neave escaped January 5, 1942. He crawled through a hole in a camp theatre to a guardhouse and marched out dressed as a German soldier. reaching Switzerland two days later.

Dutch Lieutenant Anthony Luteyn escaped January 5, 1942 with Neave.

British Lieutenant Hedley Fowler escaped September 9, 1942. Slipped out with four others through a guard office and a storeroom dressed as German officers and Polish orderlies. Only he and Van Doorninck reached Switzerland. Like Luteyn and Neave, this was another successful British Dutch effort.

Dutch Lieutenant Damiaen Joan van Doorninck escaped September 9, 1942 with Fowler.

British Capt. Patrick R. Reid escaped October 14, 1942. He slipped through the kitchen into the German yard then into the Kommandantur cellar and down to a dry moat through the park. He took four days to reach Switzerland.

Canadian Flight Lieutenant Howard D. Wardle (RAF) escaped October 14, 1942 with Reid.

British Major Ronald B. Littledale escaped October 14, 1942 with Reid.

British Lieutenant-Commander William E. Stephens escaped October 14, 1942 with Littledale.

British Lieutenant William A. Millar escaped January, 1944. He broke into a German courtyard and hid in a truck intending to go to Czechoslovakia. He never reached home and is listed missing on the Bayeux memorial. There is speculation that he was caught and executed in Mauthausen concentration camp as a victim of the secret Kugel-erlass (Bullet Decree) July 15, 1944.

French Lieutenants J. Durand-Hornus, G. de Frondeville and J. Prot escaped while on a visit to the town dentist December 17, 1941.

Polish Lieutenant Kroner was transferred to Königswartha Hospital where he jumped out of the window.

French Lieutenant Boucheron fled from Zeitz Hospital, was recaptured, and later escaped from Düsseldorf prison.

French Lieutenants Odry and Navelet escaped from Elsterhorst Hospital.

British Captain Louis Rémy escaped from Gnaschwitz military hospital. His three companions were captured, but he reached Algeciras by boat, and later Britain.

British Squadron Leader Brian Paddon escaped to Sweden via Danzig

French Lieutenant Raymond Bouillez escaped from a hospital after an unsuccessful attempt to jump from a train.

Dutch Lieutenant J. van Lynden slipped away when the Dutch were moved to Stanislau camp.

French Lieutenant A. Darthenay escaped from a hospital at Hohenstein-Ernstthal, later joined the French Resistance, and was killed by the Gestapo on April 7, 1944.

Indian RAMC Captain Birendra Nath Mazumdar M.D. was the only Indian in Colditz. He went on a hunger strike to have himself transferred into an Indian-only camp. His wish was granted three weeks later and he escaped from that camp to France and reached Switzerland in 1944 with the aid of the French Resistance.

W. E. "Wally" Hammond (from the sunken submarine HMS Shark) and Don "Tubby" Lister (from the captured submarine HMS Seal) campaigned for a transfer from Colditz, arguing that he was not an officer. He was transferred to Lamsdorf prison escaped from a Breslau work party and reached England via Switzerland in 1943.


Colditz was not the prison Goring described as 'escape proof' the officers from the allied countries showed initiative, courage and invention to prove him wrong.


THE END

{~ Mala Zimetbaum | Jewish Women's Archive

6 greatest escapes from Auschwitz in the history of the camp

W Witold Pilecki - Wikipedia

Rebecca Donner on Twitter: "#OTD My great-great-aunt Mildred H...cracy to fascist dictatorship 1/9 https://t.co/xv6YAWII

Did a Jewish Ballerina Shoot an SS Guard at Auschwitz? | Snopes.com

W Kołaczyce - Wikipedia

(7) Quora

News / Museum / Auschwitz-Birkenau

polish male names - Google Search

Life in the camp / History / Auschwitz-Birkenau

★ Bookmarks

Escapes and reports / Resistance / History / Auschwitz-Birkenau

The penal company / Punishments and executions / History / Auschwitz-Birkenau

Block 11 / Punishments and executions / History / Auschwitz-Birkenau

I escaped from Auschwitz | Holocaust | The Guardian

Facebook

W August Kowalczyk - Wikipedia

Witold Pilecki: Polish resistance hero went to Auschwitz to spy on Nazis - The Washington Post

Witold Pilecki: Auschwitz Volunteer Who Warned The World - Polish History

Witold Pilecki: Auschwitz Volunteer Who Warned The World | JW3

W Witold Pilecki - Wikipedia

W Dirlewanger Brigade - Wikipedia

Political Prisoners | Holocaust Encyclopedia

W Auschwitz Protocols - Wikipedia

Irma Grese

Reports by Auschwitz escapees / Informing the world / History / Auschwitz-Birkenau

W Związek Organizacji Wojskowej - Wikipedia

Trials of SS men from the Auschwitz Concentration Camp garrison / The SS garrison / History / Auschwitz-Birkenau

The Holocaust's Great Escape | History| Smithsonian Magazine

Witold Pilecki: the Man Who Volunteered To Go To Auschwitz

The Escape Artist by Jonathan Freedland review – how an Auschwitz breakout alerted the world | History books | The Gua

Tales from Auschwitz: survivor stories | Holocaust | The Guardian

The Struggle to Survive Auschwitz : Museum of Jewish Heritage — A Living Memorial to the Holocaust

SESSION EXPIRED

Rudolf Vrba

Stella Goldschlag Kubler – "a catcher" who identified and sent to death thousands of Jews - Justice For Polish Victims

G Alexander 'Sasha' Pechersky. - Google Search

Holocaust Historical Society

G Leon Feldhendler - Google Search

Survivors of the revolt - Sobibor Interviews

W Treblinka extermination camp - Wikipedia

Leon Feldhendler - Biography — JewAge

History & Overview of Sobibor

Holocaust Survivor Shares The Rare Moments Of Kindness Amid Unimaginable Cruelty | Kind World

Laughter in a Time of Tragedy: Examining Humor during the Holocaust

Kapos: collaborators, perpetrators or victims? - Sydney Jewish Museum

Unseen pics of Sobibór death camp shed ghastly light on Nazi horror facility – The First News

niemann solibor - Search

W List of mass escapes from German POW camps - Wikipedia

▼

Chaim Engel - Sobibor Interviews

Inspiring Stories About People Who Escaped The Holocaust

https://manoa.hawaii.edu/wcdi/projects/mapping-pow-camps/#:~:text=POW Camp Groups in Japan,-Most prisoner-of&text=

Japanese POW Camps During World War Two - History

Pictures emerge showing Japanese troops using Sikh POWs as practice targets | SBS Punjabi

W    List of prisoner-of-war escapes - Wikipedia

BRUTAL TREATMENT OF POWS BY THE JAPANESE AND ATROCITIES BY U.S. SOLDIERS | Facts and Details

Survival, Resistance, and Escape on Palawan | The National WWII Museum | New Orleans

Bataan Death March | Definition, Date, Pictures, Facts, Survivors, & Significance | Britannica

W    Selarang Barracks Incident - Wikipedia

W    Samuel Grashio - Wikipedia

'Dispose of Them': Massacre of American POWs in the Philippines | The National WWII Museum | New Orleans

Breavington & Gale — Historic War Tours

Soldier boldly faced his firing squad

75th anniversary of the liberation of Changi | Australian War Memorial

⊘ BRUTAL TREATMENT OF POWS BY THE JAPANESE AND ATROCITIES BY U.S. SOLDIERS | Facts and Details ⋮

▪ Survival, Resistance, and Escape on Palawan | The National WWII Museum | New Orleans   https://www.nationalww2museum.org/war/articles... ⋮

▦ Bataan Death March | Definition, Date, Pictures, Facts, Survivors, & Significance | Britannica ⋮

W Selarang Barracks incident - Wikipedia ⋮

W Samuel Grashio - Wikipedia ⋮

▪ 'Dispose of Them': Massacre of American POWs in the Philippines | The National WWII Museum | New Orleans ⋮

⚘ Breavington & Gale — Historic War Tours ⋮

⑤ Soldier boldly faced his firing squad ⋮

▲ 75th anniversary of the liberation of Changi | Australian War Memorial ⋮

▦ Survivors of the revolt - Sobibor Interviews

W Treblinka extermination camp - Wikipedia

🕎 Leon Feldhendler - Biography — JewAge

⚑ History & Overview of Sobibor

▪ Holocaust Survivor Shares The Rare Moments Of Kindness Amid Unimaginable Cruelty | Kind World

D Laughter in a Time of Tragedy: Examining Humor during the Holocaust

⋓ Kapos: collaborators, perpetrators or victims? - Sydney Jewish Museum

🕏 Unseen pics of Sobibór death camp shed ghastly light on Nazi horror facility — The First News

Q niemann solibor - Search

W List of mass escapes from German POW camps - Wikipedia

Ⓜ 'Escapes'. Episode 2. The great escape from KL Lublin - Majdanek

▦ Lublin | Poland | Britannica

▪ Remembering the Sobibor Uprising | The National WWII Museum | New Orleans

W Selma Engel-Wijnberg - Wikipedia

▦ Chaim Engel - Sobibor Interviews

⚘ Inspiring Stories About People Who Escaped The Holocaust

◎ https://manoa.hawaii.edu/wcdi/projects/mapping-pow-camps/#:~:text=POW Camp Groups in Japan,-Most priso

Ⓗ Japanese POW Camps During World War Two - History

⚑ Pictures emerge showing Japanese troops using Sikh POWs as practice targets | SBS Punjabi

W List of prisoner-of-war escapes - Wikipedia

⊘ BRUTAL TREATMENT OF POWS BY THE JAPANESE AND ATROCITIES BY U.S. SOLDIERS | Facts and Details

First published 2023 by Crabtree Pty Ltd

All rights reserved.

No part of this publication may be reproduced, stored in a retrieval system, or transmitted in any form or any means electronic, mechanical, photocopying, recording or otherwise without the prior permission of the publisher.

Copyright © Crabtree Pty Ltd 2023

ISBN: 978-0-6459087-0-1 (p/b)
ISBN: 978-0-6459087-1-8 (ebook)

www.ingramcontent.com/pod-product-compliance
Lightning Source LLC
Chambersburg PA
CBHW030531020726
47494CB00004B/1308